Holograms of Fear

Slavenka Drakulić

HOLOGRAMS OF FEAR

A NOVEL

W · W · NORTON & COMPANY

New York   London

Printed in the United States of America

Manufacturing by The Maple-Vail Manufacturing Group.

ISBN: 0-393-03107-2

W. W. Norton & Company, Inc.
500 Fifth Avenue, New York, N.Y. 10110
W. W. Norton & Company, Ltd
10 Coptic Street, London WC1A 1PU

1 2 3 4 5 6 7 8 9 0

Karl Pribram: Sir John Eccles mentioned in an article several years ago that 'synaptic potentials' – the electrical exchanges between brain cells – don't occur alone. Every nerve branches, and when the electrical message goes down the branches, a ripple, or a wave front, is formed. When other wave fronts come to the same location from other directions the wave fronts intersect and set up an interference pattern. It's somewhat like the meeting of ripples that form around two pebbles thrown into a pond.

It seemed plausible to me that if there are interfering wave fronts in the brain, those fronts might have the same properties as a hologram. Both holograms and brain tissues can be cut up without removing their image-processing capabilities. Holograms are resistant to damage – like memory in the brain. The persistent puzzle of a distributed memory might be solved. The brain had to behave, in part, like a hologram.

Psychology Today
February 1978

HOLOGRAMS OF FEAR

Of course I was afraid.

I was afraid the whole time.

'Who can we contact should anything happen?' asked the nurse at the hospital reception desk, her head bent over the computer sheet she was filling out with a blue biro. First name, last name, date of birth (here she glanced over at me – did I seem older? younger? what?), address, telephone number. Then the letters of my long, foreign name cramped into the little, square boxes on the paper. They hardly fit. It's two o'clock in the morning. The room is lit by a single, bluish neon tube: small, white, no windows.

There is nothing personal in here, it's a no man's room, I thought as I leant against the wall. There was an excess of air in my stomach and an emptiness in my head, suddenly weightless, as if my feet were not touching the floor. I urgently needed something solid to hold on to: the table edge, the arm of a chair, a door knob, a hand.

But I came alone.

The nurse is fidgeting on her chair, too narrow for her heavy, meaty body. Under the table she spreads her legs for balance, as if a special effort is required to stay sitting at this time of night. One of her feet is bare, its shoe lying awkwardly to one side.

The scene made my stomach ache.

She's awake because of me, I thought, with a flash of guilt. I'm responsible for dragging her out of bed, for her exhaustion and the shoe that rubbed.

With that doughy white hand, a sunken gold band on the middle finger, she types in my nationality (yes, she had been to Germany with her husband, they would go again, she adores Europe – Europe, Yugoslavia, it's all the same as far as she's concerned . . .). Green letters flicker on the screen and a message says that everything is all right.

A hospital at night offers a deceptive illusion of serenity, a sense that nothing particular is happening, although up there people are sweating and flinching in their sleep, shrieking, wheezing, lights are being turned on and off. The dull thud of footsteps, someone moans. Here on the ground floor nothing of that can be heard. I can relax, nestle into the half-dark serenity.

I'd arrived.

It was my third winter running in Boston. Something would happen, I promised myself, something had to happen. One fine day the computer would print out your name, the phone would ring, and you, half doubting, would say: 'Finally!' Calmly, since that was what you had been waiting for, you would go to the hospital. Quickly – it had to be quick – they'd operate. And then you'd get on with real life.

But no, no, I didn't imagine the future like that. I didn't

2

imagine it at all. Not even the operation. I thought only of the bracelet, how I'd put the plastic strip with my name and number around my wrist and breathe a sigh of relief. It would be the end of fear, a sign that the system does function. One fine day . . .

The day is not fine. It is Thursday, a chilly February wind is blowing, the quiet humming of the ventilation system can be heard and the nurse, her head raised in expectation, says: 'Well?'

I am dumb. It has happened.

The fact that I am sitting here and the thin strip is around my hand means as much. In New York I got on to the last plane for Boston that night. That was last night. So long ago, I thought and felt uncomfortable. Time thickened to a dense mass of uncertainty, now expanding and grabbing me from inside.

'I couldn't live like that,' Jelena said.

I had no choice. Every other morning at five o'clock I went for my dialysis at the hospital on 72nd Street. I didn't consider the possibility of not going. The healthy can choose. Life is simple when you're sick, as it is for people in jail or in the army. There are rules that are more than rules because breaking them can only mean one thing. At first this is non-freedom but later, it is just certainty.

Yesterday morning was not particularly special. I went out in front of the house and took a deep breath of frozen air. I could almost bite it, like thin glass. The frost on the trees along the side of Central Park was glistening although daybreak was nowhere in sight; the light along the tree tops came from nowhere. An icy film covered the sidewalk. The

3

main entrance to the hospital was locked. I went to the back door, behind the parking lot and the garbage cans. The doorman was drowsing. The elevator door closed after me on the third floor, like an airlock shutting over my head. I descended into another reality like a submarine. I entered the room. Here secret alchemical tests are run that the people upstairs know nothing about. People come into the room and lie down on the beds. Nurses attach them with needles and tubes to box-like machines on spidery chrome stands that suck up their blood. A few hours later, slightly groggy, those people slowly get up from their beds and go out into the light of day, and no one knows that they have just arrived from another, underwater world in which their blood has passed through a machine several hundred times, pushing through the slender fibres of the filter, until it returns to the body, cleansed. There are no witnesses. Witnesses are rare and they are not easily granted access. Their eyes full of mute questions and a panicky fear of blood.

Here the blood flows in streams: in veins, capillaries, pumps, rubber hoses, in clear plastic tubes, in cylindrical dishes with filters. As if the white room was woven with a red web. Everyone is quiet, deathly tired. They communicate in code, in subdued tones. The nurses go from bed to bed – upholstered in brown plastic, cracked along the edges, that sticks to your skin – and repeat the procedure: wipe the place on your arm with alcohol, poke in the needle, attach it to the tube, turn on the machine, then watch closely as the blood, foaming at the top, fills the container and the thin, white fibres.

4

A choreographed path in the vestibule of . . . death.

That gaping, waxy vacuum.

Almost nothing can be heard. An uneasy nothing, except for the humming. Is it the hum of the machine or the coursing of blood? The windowpanes are milky, white glass. Traces of the outside world only come in through the television set, like a crack in the space. But they are distant images.

The needle pierces the vein of the inside of my elbow with a little resistance. I relax. The next four hours I can doze, listening to footsteps, the humming of the blood pumps, the creak of equipment being moved about, the TV announcer's voice as he says: 'Good morning, America.' I feel pretty good. I'm safe. I will lie here patiently and quietly, with a needle in my right arm, attached to the arm of the chair, covered with a yellow cotton blanket on which I can see traces of washed-out blood. Then I'll be free for a full thirty-six hours.

The door of the room is the boundary. Time spent in this room somehow doesn't count. It is not added, because it is always the same; or it's figured differently, like an interruption or a pause. I don't make a secret of it. I don't try to hide it. I say, 'I am going for dialysis now,' but it's a strange word, like psoriasis or menopause, a medical term with no image or experience behind it. It doesn't convey this hospital room, the electricity powering the machines, the needle approaching my arm, the coming and going, the time between. It is hard to understand. My friends were horrified for a while, then forgot.

I myself often have the feeling that it is happening to

someone else, to a different me. I split, I visibly split. I have
to function. So I split into Me and my body, the two separated by a fine, taut membrane of indifference. The body
becomes an extension of the machine, yet that dependency
is not disturbing. It doesn't obsess me, that's just how
it is.

I've been split for years – five? six? – it's easier that way.
Sometimes I wonder about where it began. It is difficult to
pinpoint. The disease suddenly appeared in my ancestors'
genes. Who was the first? Perhaps my grandfather. While
still quite young, he stopped eating and would only drink.
He grew paler and paler, his legs began to swell until his
skin was so stretched that it began to crack. Then he
vomited up a murky yellow liquid and the stench of urine
spread from his mouth. He died exhausted, bloated, perhaps in his sleep.

His son remembered a high, moist brow and a smell that
lingered in the house for days.

The thing moved from person to person like bad luck.
No one could tell who it would attack. It attacked my
father. It attacked me. It left my brother unharmed. We
almost thought that it had skipped us, too, that those
ancestors who had died in the past had nothing to do with
us. But at the first signs – nausea, vomiting, tiredness – I
knew that it had come. The doctors didn't tell me right
away although they suspected it. I was already pale, my
pulse was fast and every time I lay down I thought I might
not be able to get up. Later my father came down with it as
well. They told us that these days it was possible to live
with it, that there were machines, kidney transplants.

Various deals could be struck with the sickness, negotiating with bad luck.

I have been negotiating for years.

The split makes it possible to distinguish between the two realities. What's happening to me now, here, in this capsule outside time, has nothing to do with my other life. The first reality is on the surface: streets, stores, window displays, friends, lunch, typewriter, the unexpected. Like that afternoon meeting with Sharon in the tea parlour at Hotel Le Cirque, after I emerged from the submarine. The black lace stockings I was wearing were in sharp contrast to the morning's experience. What's the sense in putting on black lace stockings after spending four hours attached to a machine that rinses out your deepest insides? Black lace stockings make sense in only one of those two realities, surrounded by elegant red velvet and golden trim on the arm chairs, under subdued lighting and imitation art nouveau ceilings. Should I so desire I can, at a moment's notice, summon another reality – the room, the bed, the smell of alcohol, the waxed floor. Side by side, they would make a charming, dramatic contrast. Velvet next to plastic, gold next to steel. I don't want to do that. To mix realities would mean to get lost. To question one because of the other.

Sharon wore a scarf over her hair and fine, pale pink leather gloves. Grease was dripping down her gloves from a carelessly wrapped hamburger and on to the book she handed me. She wiped her gloves on the linen napkin that had been draped over the teapot. Then her gloved hand brought the brimming teacup to her lips. Her skin was perfectly transparent. Pouting lips with clearly defined edges, light eyes, a little indifferent. She spoke of her new book with the false indifference of someone repeating something for the hundredth time. Who knows how long she'd been practising this pose. She was healthy, she strolled around in daytime, ate hamburgers, sipped teas, coke, water, inhabited the first reality. But in spite of it all, anxiety flickered across her transparent face for a moment.

I turned to look away. I couldn't stand to see it. The conversation was meant to protect me, to give me a sense of safety, the hope that it is possible to live without the split, without fear.

In the Boston hospital the nurse asks me again: 'Well?'

Something in her voice, the way she looks at me with raised eyebrows, slightly startled by my silence, puts me on edge. 'Should anything happen . . .' The way she says it drains all my serenity, carefully hoarded since the night before. What did that 'should' mean? Now that I have made it this far, when every unexpected turn of events has been eliminated.

A light shudder down my spine. Is it a premonition of fear? Not after everything, not now. Fear was something to be faced a long time ago, when the decision was made, when you accepted the possibility of an operation, when you allowed yourself that kind of hope. Now it is too late for fear, for any kind of feeling. Best to sink into emptiness, into silence. Submit to the hospital routine, doubt nothing. But I might just get up and walk out. I have seen it – people who gave up at the last minute, at the door of the operating theatre. They didn't have the strength for such an irrevocable decision. Late fall, the face of a woman in the neighbouring bed, her muted sobbing after a night spent awake. In a few hours she had to decide. First she said yes, then no. Her explanation was a single word: fear.

Fear of pain. Fear of the unknown. Fear of death.

Dialysis is something familiar. It is a firm system, an established framework of life that offers certainty, rhythm. Every other day you must go to the hospital at a certain time, get into pyjamas and lie in a bed and then spend four hours attached to a machine. The blood is surprisingly, unnaturally pale. It is impossible to watch that scene every other day and think of death. It is impossible to live with the terrifying nightmare that the slender plastic tubes could snap, that the blood might flood the worn-out linoleum floor, spray the walls, flow down the hospital corridors and out into the yard, like a strange, dark stream, narrower and narrower, until it becomes a trickle and then soaks into the ground. After a while the pumps, tubes and machines melt into the discreet décor like faded flowers on hotel wallpaper. You must survive the minutes and hours. Will the needle prick be more or less painful? Should I sleep or read the paper? Will there be crêpes for supper? The fear of death, when crumbled into small daily rations, becomes quite bearable. It is important that all elements are familiar and predictable, that the faces of the nurses are always the same, the arrangement of the beds identical and the rhythm of coming and going unchanged.

But the faces of the people attached to the machines change from time to time. They disappear. Their death is not something unexpected. It too is part of the familiar system. The body wastes away from day to day, slowly, but nonetheless so visibly that it seems inevitable and logical. Like an accelerated movie sequence of ageing: the skin grows more wrinkled, first yellowish, then brown and leathery, as if tanned. The hands become knotted, the posture bent, unsure. You get used to it, to your own daily dying, disintegration crumbled into minutes. It is easier than to imagine the sudden change that an operation brings. An operation eliminates the familiar and places a person in an entirely new situation. Decisions must be made, risks taken, uncertainty, pain and the unknown endured.

Fear surfaces, suddenly. Bursting whole from within, turning into a high wall that seems impossible to climb. Looking at it paralyses all movement. It surrounds you on all sides. If you move to examine it, touch its smooth, slippery surface, its texture, height, bulk, you are certain not to master it. Do not waver. Close your eyes and jump.

Into the dark, as into water.

Seeing me hesitate, the nurse tries to comfort me. She covers my clenched fist with her hand and says: 'It's for the computer, you know.' Her touch reassures me, though that disturbing 'should' had already settled in the pit of my stomach as if I had eaten earth. A feeling of undefined danger, the presence of a threat.

Indeed, who could they contact 'should anything happen'? The people I know in New York? The friend in Cambridge with whom I'm staying? And what would they do then?

Or should the hospital contact my daughter, Natasha? Thursday. Early morning in an empty house. Outside it would still be dark. Natasha gets up, puts milk on to warm, flips on the light in the bathroom and turns on the heating. The radio fills the empty house with sound, and the start of that dark winter Thursday immediately seems promising. Then the telephone rings.

Or perhaps this nurse, or a doctor or someone whose job it is to do so would wake my mother up in the middle of the night. The telephone would ring for a long time. She would get up and sneak out quietly so as not to disturb my father who had finally conquered sleep. Shivering and feeling her way through the dark she would look for her woollen shawl to cover her shoulders. Then she would pick up the receiver and the voice at the other end would not be mine. Someone would say: 'You have a call from Boston.' The line would be bad as usual, full of hiss and crackle. The ocean would sound in the receiver and an unknown voice in a foreign language would begin: 'This is New England Deaconess Hospital in Boston . . .' She doesn't understand English, but she would recognise bad news.

No, not my mother or my daughter.

I should have brought someone with me, someone who could have answered the questions instead of me, filled out the questionnaires, held me by the hand, shattered with their voice the unbearable silence of the reception desk. Someone I could have told about the fear slowly growing in my stomach, in my feet now sticking to the floor, in my sweating hands, in my furtive gaze examining the bars of this cage, in the distinctive odour of fear, in all the signs that appear within the body while the brain, still emptied, awakens.

I should have let Grace come with me. She would have taken my mind off it. The operation is outside my control. She knows my hysterical need to keep everything under control. Dismay when I think that because of the anaesthetic I won't know what is happening to me, that it will all go on outside my consciousness, my only protection. If I could talk about it it would be easier.

If Jelena were here, she would quickly convince me that there is no reason to be worried. Everything is running as smoothly as possible, she'd tell me: 'You might not have received the message. They might not have found you in time. What if you'd been late for the last plane? What if a snowstorm had come up, or you'd had the flu?' So many unforeseeable factors could have happened. 'Actually, you're lucky,' she'd say. At the word luck, I would laugh.

Or Ivan. But he could never be here, I realised that three years ago when I came to this hospital for the first time. I was on dialysis. In the next bed lay a very pale, frightened man. Next to him sat a woman. She held his hand. She didn't let it go for hours. 'Stay calm,' she whispered, 'I'm here by your side.' He tossed and turned fretfully in bed, crumpling the sheet with his free right hand. 'I can't stand it, I can't stand it,' he kept repeating. I was suddenly afraid he might be dying but no, the nurses said cheerfully, the young man has just been assigned a kidney and in a few hours he'll be operated on. He was blind. They had a small child. The woman sat there patiently and didn't let go of his hand, as if her hand was the thread, the bond with something living outside this room, a trusty guiding thread.

If I am ever faced with an operation, I thought then, Ivan

won't be by my side. I wanted to cry, but I didn't: while I was able to cope alone, he took no interest in my underwater realm. He couldn't bear to hear me talk of the sickness. He'd get up from the table abruptly, without a word. Silence glittering on the smooth surface between us. When he left, I didn't stop him. I knew that I would be more and more alone as time passed. A wall grew up around me. I carefully stuffed all the holes and cracks through which another being could enter, leaving only one passage open to Natasha. All my emotional energy was channelled towards her as if supply was limited and the way I spent it determined how long it would last. I had to economise.

Perhaps I was proud that I would die such a brave, lonely death. One day the wall will simply be high enough and all the holes so well stopped that darkness will finally reign inside. No one will be able to get in. I will no longer be able to get out. I wouldn't even want to. But that was not true. The slightest knock and everything would have come tumbling down. My construct was idealistic, falsely noble, heroic. Perhaps I even enjoyed it. It protected me from myself. As long as consciousness and imagination functioned, as long as images appeared, even as I imagined my own demise, I was sure of what I was.

Anxiety surges to my throat, the wall comes tumbling down and, utterly exposed in the bluish neon light, I ache for people I have trusted, even briefly. The husbands, lovers, friends. A touch, a face, a voice. An armour is melting. Last night's impertinent assertion that I could manage on my own seems so unjust, as if someone else thought it up to punish me.

It is still not too late. There are two telephones in the bright, polished corridor, I noticed them when I arrived. I can get up, take a few steps to the blue box on the wall, lift the receiver, dial a number and say: 'I am alone, I can't go on, say something, let me hear your voice. Say that this is a nightmare, a bad dream that will pass. I'm afraid that I've wandered into the wrong life, that I've put on someone else's shoes. A fatal error has been made – I know it but there is no one I can tell. Why is my body perspiring, trembling, almost weightless, fragile? This is happening to some other, unknown Me that has suddenly surfaced and discovered my long-concealed weakness. If I hear a familiar voice it will convince me that I still exist, that I am real. That this split is only temporary . . .' To avoid facing myself once and for all. With my solitude. With fear.

A voice, all I need is a voice.

It's late.

I can't get up, I can't call, I can't do anything anymore. In the silent reception my cracked voice would bounce off the walls and come back to me like an empty echo. The slightest move and something unforeseen will happen. I might vomit right there on the desk, on the papers, on the computer, on the nurse's round knees. Or I'll faint. Or I'll burst into loud sobs.

'I don't have anyone,' I say, looking into her eyes. 'I am alone.'

'Don't you have a husband?'

'No, I don't.'

'Or children?'

'No.'

'Parents, friends, neighbours?'

I stopped answering. How could I explain it to her: all of them are way up there, on the surface. My voice can't reach them. There is water between us.

At about eight o'clock yesterday evening I still didn't know. I took a cab to a dinner. 'Harlem no good place,' the taxi driver protested, a little Chinese man who could hardly see over the steering wheel. He kept peering around, moving through the darkness flashing with glowing bar fronts. He stopped in front of Sylvia's Restaurant on Lenox Avenue across from a row of parked limousines with dark windows and motionless chauffeurs. When I stepped out on to the sidewalk I thought – for no reason – that the doorman wouldn't let me in. It was an invitation-only dinner and I was late. I fingered the piece of stiff card in my pocket thinking: no, this is not the problem. I was so nervous I almost stumbled. I was certain there was something conspicuous about me, some detail that would let everyone know I'm not part of this world. Perhaps blood was oozing through the plaster on my arm? No. Maybe my coat that I'd bought for three dollars on Canal Street?

It was raining. I bought the coat and ran into a Chinese restaurant. I sat next to the window and ordered noodles. On the table stood a red plastic napkin dispenser, filthy from flies, with black finger and soy sauce smudges. It suddenly seemed as if a membrane were snapping, that something was gushing darkly upward, leaving a dark, sticky smudge on the box, on my noodles with black mushrooms. My gaze is getting sticky, I thought, dirtying the things around it. It's obvious, it must be obvious.

But the doorman nodded as if I were his personal guest and, encouraged, I went in.

The glass doors were steamy and drops slid down the frame to the floor. I caught sight of Grace through the soft mist, her face melting at the edges. She came towards me, parted the dense crowd of people with her hands as if swimming through water that was holding her back.

That took a long time.

Suddenly I am in the middle of the crowd. Grace is holding me firmly by the shoulder. She is talking. Shouting.

'What is going on?'

She opens her mouth. I can't hear anything.

'Why are you shouting?'

She shouts even louder.

'Let me go!'

Then I finally hear her voice, coming from a distance.

'You've got to leave right away, travel, the operation will be at six in the morning.'

'No,' I said. 'No. No.'

Perhaps I shouted. I must have started to cry. That slimy, sticky anxiety, that unbearable double burden burst to the surface. Black. All I could see was blackness – black, blurred shadows, a black hole sucking me in. Grace held me tightly. 'Don't be afraid, I won't let you go alone,' she said.

I knew it would happen, that the two realities would clash.

Now they have.

It should have happened differently, not in a restaurant. It is so stupid. A long table, people I should be talking to, to tell them about the ... they would have inevitably asked about the situation in Europe, about Poland, the position of the intellectual under socialism, and is it true that ...

What does the operation have to do with this restaurant, with people debating about future projects while carefully bringing forkfuls of meat to their mouths? They know. Now, they know. Grace is speaking excitedly and waving her hands. She is pointing to me. They are staring at me between bites. How many? Five? Eight? I feel the sickness pouring out of me on all sides, slopping on to their plates, exposing itself in all its nakedness and perversity. They suddenly see the veins through which pulsates a filtered salty solution, not blood. An anthropomorphic machine covered with a thin layer of artificial skin, cracking at the seams. A woman wearing a hat wipes her mouth with a napkin, gets up and shakes my hand.

'Congratulations,' she says.

My mouth is dry.

I want to say something, explain. 'No. You haven't understood – what you are looking at, this machine, it isn't me. I am crouching inside, hidden, humiliated, because I don't know how to defend myself.'

But all I say is: 'Thank you.'

How can I explain the double system: anticipation and despair, hope and fear? How can I tell them about my permanent high wire act, strung way up above the ground, trying to keep my balance.

Balancing is my job.

Now it is no longer possible.

I knew that the summons to the operation could arrive

at any time, but it should have happened without witnesses, in a situation that I could control. Not here, with the world fractured into unconnected images: doors that open and shut, white tiles glistening on a kitchen wall, an empty table by the bar, a hand pouring beer. There is no whole. My eyes no longer see the whole. A string of images that are repeated, first slowly and then faster and faster.

Slow down, it should slow down.

A hand pushes me into a taxi. Grace. She says: 'I'm coming with you.' I gruffly push her aside. Her open palms stay glued for a moment to the car window, as if she wants to touch my face in parting. She'll catch cold, I think, standing there in a thin white blouse with a low back. She stands on the sidewalk and doesn't know what to do with herself, small, now quite far away.

Do I have time?

First I have to change. How would it seem if I were to arrive at the hospital in black lace stockings and patent leather shoes? As if I didn't care, maybe frivolous. Magenta lipstick, red hair – foolish. I need to wear something suitable, practical (words right out of a fashion magazine). The green sweater, that colour suits me. Or sporty, my running suit, like I'm going out for some exercise. Well, actually I am going for exercise. And I'll need a bathrobe. I don't have one. On purpose I never bought one. It must be twenty years ago that I heard a story about a woman who went out and bought all the things she would need for her baby and it was stillborn. She had tempted fate. My baby was, luckily, born a month premature. The evening before, a Saturday, I was at a wedding (I remember that it was Saturday, because weddings are usually held on Saturdays in Zagreb). I had no idea that I'd be having a baby the next day. Snow fell in the morning – quite early, November 10th – and I watched the flakes out of the obstetrics ward window, thinking how good it was that I hadn't gotten any diapers.

Once again I was rushing to the hospital. I stare indecisively out of the window at the skyscraper on West 63rd Street. I wonder what precisely I should be doing?

Sort things out. Take things one step at a time. I didn't prepare anything, buy anything, organise anything. Do I have time? I haven't washed my hair. Do I have time? Toothbrush, make-up, underwear – so little. Suddenly I feel I haven't enough, that in the hospital room surrounded by unknown things I will get completely lost. I pick up things from the table and stuff them into my bag: books, paper, a lot of paper, pencils, notes, an unfinished article – elements of the coordinate system. It will be so good to lie in bed in peace and quiet and read and think. The operation has already turned into a technical detail, something unquestionable, almost simple.

'Would you like to eat something?' Mira asks.

Should I eat? Is that reality? What criteria should I use to decide? An intolerable situation. I can't eat and not eat at the same time, follow two lines of contradictory instructions. Mira and Davor press me to make up my mind, to go if I'm going, if I want to budge. Two pieces of bread and butter and a glass of beer are standing on the oval table covered with a white tablecloth on a black eight-sided plate. A knife. Butter. Salt. An ashtray with one butt. A vase. I eat. The trip, it will just be a longish trip, nothing special, this isn't the first time that I have had to leave in such a hurry. *Don't think twice, don't think twice, tra la la*, the refrain runs round my head like a little scribbled note, part of the hit song I picked up along the way at the bar, in the taxi, on television.

Mira follows me into the bathroom and then into the kitchen.

'You must hurry,' she says, 'you haven't much time.' She looks at me, worried, sad. My feet are growing weaker and weaker. I must sit down. It is late. I am tired.

'I wish I could go to sleep,' I tell her.

With my head resting on the table, I know that it isn't possible, that I can do nothing at this point but go.

In the taxi to the airport, Mira keeps repeating: 'Don't worry, everything will be fine, everything will be fine.' I do worry, though, that the taxi will be late, that I won't have enough money, that the plane will be delayed. I breathe in a little fresh air, as if I have been sentenced and am on my way to jail. The night is clear. I don't know when I'll be out.

The airplane is late.

Maybe I can still do something for myself and pronounce out loud the words of fear sticking to the roof of my mouth. The clock in the airport waiting room shows that it is eleven o'clock. I call Ana. I hear her voice. She is standing in a narrow, messy kitchen, legs astride, as if about to suddenly take a ballet step, forgetting that she is making dinner – a roast chicken and avocado salad, perhaps a soufflé, her standard fare. She holds the telephone receiver with her shoulder. The kitchen has no door. There are glass jars in rows on the open shelves above her head with flour, sugar, pasta, rice and spices. They are covered with dust. She takes them down all the time, adds salt or flour, tomato paste, marjoram. I tell her that I am at the airport. 'Why did you decide to leave so suddenly? You didn't mention it before.'

I think about how the roaches have hidden under her feet in the cracks of the wooden floor. They wait for her to leave and turn off the light so they can descend upon the bread basket, the fruit and the black coffee grounds in the cups. I can see them creeping all over the wooden kitchen counter, tiny, quick, red. When I saw them for the first time on a piece of bread that I was holding, I felt as if the unchewed lump of food was coming back into my mouth. Ana laughed and tapped the bread. Otherwise they would crunch unpleasantly under the teeth, she said. I think of them with tenderness.

Ana's voice is suspicious. Why are you travelling?

The operation.

Silence. Silence rustled in the receiver. Passengers are already boarding.

Ana says: 'I'm so happy!'

I drink a few sips of Coke on the plane. It's too sweet. It seems out of proportion to notice so much detail all of a sudden. A thread had been pulled out of the orange fabric on the seat in front of me. The tie on the man in the next seat was crooked. I wanted to straighten it, but I overcame the impulse. I looked out the window. What if the plane were to crash right now? I thought about it with indifference, as if everything was already happening to someone else.

It is four o'clock in the morning. At the end of the corridor someone has turned on a light. Small, sharp steps can be heard. Another nurse comes in, takes my arm and leads me to the room as if I am chronically ill. I will wait there.

'You will wait here,' she says on the way out.

The light glares on the yellow walls. In the middle is a metal bed. Why didn't the nurse close the door? Is she afraid that I'll howl, smash my head against the wall, dig tiles up from the floor with my fingernails or write out secret messages in blood on the bathroom wall? What do other people do at times like this?

All trace of earlier residents had been carefully removed from the smooth tiled walls, the tidy bed, the bedside table, lamp, clothing closet and washbasin. No one spends enough time here to leave a visible, palpable trace: only stale air that hints at yesterday's odour, a past, old odour, a reliable sign that someone touched the borderline here, not so long ago, between themselves and the void.

The nurse came in again and looked at me with pity. She didn't say anything. She didn't try to comfort me. With sure, practised movements she measured my blood pressure, took some blood, did an ECG. I was so obviously, so nakedly alone that I was ashamed in front of her. She did everything quickly, without stopping, as if my loneliness bothered her, too.

'What did you have for dinner?'

'Bread and butter. Beer.'

'This will be easy,' she said, inserting the enema tube carefully, gently. At least the way in which she treated my body inspired a little trust. The certainty that there was a

customary, established routine that was part of the procedure. She sealed my documents in a paper envelope and
took the clothes. Pants. Green sweater. Boots. Coat. I can
no longer change my mind.

Would they return my clothes afterwards?

She nodded.

Afterwards? After what? The word bounces like a ball in
my brain, a leaden ball that cannot find a place to settle
into. I do not believe that I could say it, I mean seriously
say it. There is no afterwards, there is only now. But the
word has already been said. 'After.' Does it really exist? I
want it to exist.

Longing erupts suddenly, like dizziness.

I am growing calmer. Or so it seems to me. Control has
been re-established, if you can call this state of emptiness
control. I can talk with the anaesthetist with utter com-
posure (it must be the last visit, I am beginning to wish it
were six o'clock, already), a dark-skinned little man with a
pointy head who hops nervously round the room like an
elegant toreador or a dancer. The nurse takes another ECG.
The anaesthetist questions me on past heart problems and I
try hard to remember whether there was anything. I am so
tired. I would like to sleep, sleep at last. His rhythmic
movements and voice are lulling me to sleep. But I mustn't
sleep, I shall not. I have to think back. He says that it's important. There was something last summer – pain, nausea –
but it passed, I forgot about it.

Is it important now?

'Tell me everything you can remember. Describe in detail
what you felt. Nausea? Tension? Did you vomit? Did you go

23

to hospital immediately? Why not?'

For the first time he looks carefully at my face.

'I am quite sure that it was a minor heart attack,' he says and repeats that it is important to remember every detail, especially when it happened. This will dictate whether I am given a total anaesthetic or just a shot to the spine after which I will feel no pain but will be aware of everything.

So, a heart attack. I'm no longer so certain that this is happening to someone else. My smart little controlled mechanism is not functioning so smoothly. It is halting, wearing dangerously down. It crept up and jumped me when I was least prepared. I glance at his dry, dark fingers pressing the stethoscope to my chest and can remember everything.

Sunday afternoon. Voices heard from the garden. A tram passes. The air heavy with the fragrance of roses and mint. Blood pounding in my temples from the heat. I go to the bathroom. As my damp hand passes across my face, I break out in a cold sweat.

Pain, like a blow, then a dull reverberation that spreads through my left arm, my shoulder blade, my sternum. I describe the blow to the anaesthetist, the pain piercing my chest like a dagger.

'Is that called a heart attack?'

He nods.

The weight of the unspoken burden, accumulated for years, assuming the form of a physical sign, a feeling that I might burst apart, as if my flesh might open and expose my insides, my guts, my heart – that red lump that swells because it can no longer bear it.

How was it I could speak at Nina's funeral?

I had to. Others didn't have the strength. She couldn't go off like that without a word. There was some shade in front of the mortuary. Small shocked groups of people stood motionless in the shade of the maple trees. A man next to me said 'Why?' so loudly that people nearby turned their heads to look away, as if death had touched them with his word.

Her relatives stood in a semicircle by her coffin in the stuffy chapel, sheltered by the flowers. The father quite calm, just a little hunched. I can't remember what I said, I was thinking of him. He had to break down her doors. First one then the other. Before that he rang the bell a long time, but she gave no answer.

To find your child as she lies there alone, cold, in a little room – it was dark, when he got in, the evening of the following day.

To call the ambulance, the police.

To watch as they pack her into a black plastic body bag; the zipper slips upward over the stomach, breast, face, hair.

To lock the door of her apartment, to go home and tell her mother.

Afterwards they asked me how could I speak so effortlessly at my friend's funeral. That afternoon she had been at my place, drunk a glass of wine and then gone home and poisoned herself with gas. I put on a new, black silk dress. I went to the hairdresser, applied my make-up carefully and wore the earrings she had given me for my birthday. I didn't cry, I didn't cry at all. And while for the first time in my life I made the farewell speech, a short morose monologue before the procession began, bitterness welled up inside: in a plot against myself I had intended this role for her. She would urge me to stay calm; should anything happen, Nina would look after my child. She was an accomplice in the preparations. Preparations I was constantly making for my own funeral. It could happen at any time. We needed to talk about it seriously. I was furious at her unkept promise. She beat me to it, betrayed me, gone without explanation. She sits in an armchair across the room from me, wearing olive green linen pants and shirt. She'd bought them two days before.

'I bought them two days ago. How do you like them?'

Her blonde hair was pulled back in a short ponytail. She looked young.

She smoothed the arm of the chair.

'Yes,' I said, 'they suit you.'

She looked at me hesitantly as if doubting what I said. Had she already made up her mind?

When someone takes a decision like that, does it happen gradually? Did she simply add together all the different facets of her life and keep coming up with the same, wrong total?

While I walked along by the coffin it seemed inconceivable that this was all that was left of her. I saw her light grey eyes again, how she would bite her lower lip when nervous. A sharp image embossed on the shimmering blue sky.

No, that could not be all.

I was not completely taken by surprise. Suicide had been in the air for months. She claimed that the only sure, painless and quick way was to slip the hair dryer into the bathtub while taking a bath. Let it fall in, almost by accident, since putting it in takes courage. She said that suicide is the only reasonable act in a state of total depression. She theorised about it and talked about the deaths she had seen. She suffered from insomnia. Zagreb winters are long and tedious. This last winter it seemed that she was losing her footing. She'd sit at home not even able to read. She didn't complain, she merely grew absent. She interrupted conversations, as if they disgusted her. When a young man, an acquaintance, threw himself through a window, she said: 'That spurred me on.' I heard her say those words but dismissed them with a flick of the wrist. 'Why tell me? I need courage to survive. Every other day I spend four hours hooked up to a machine.

'Do you understand? A machine!' I said furiously. 'For me, suicide is a luxury.'

I didn't know how to communicate my solitude or my vulnerability to her. To show her would mean to admit them to myself. Each of us thought that the other was better off. It was no good trying to convince her that having a child cannot be the only reason keeping me from crossing that border, so palpable in its presence. She was healthy and free and, if reasons had to be sought, those were good reasons for living. But there are no real reasons for living. She knew that and in the end no longer made any more excuses. She simply decided that she could not go on.

Then she had only to master the fear.

For some time after it happened I suffered from a sense of guilt. Not because she had gone and I – ailing and worn as I am, always on the verge, always in certain but invisible

27

danger – stayed behind, but because I was angry at her. This worried me. If I had truly come to terms with death, as I thought I had, why the bitterness and anxiety? Something in her death unsettled me: the closeness, perhaps the decisiveness; or the giving up, the ease of giving up. Nina brought me close to the edge of the abyss and made me realise how easy it is to jump. Suddenly a possibility opened up that I had completely excluded, that I had despised because I was afraid (it spurred her on, she mentioned it spurring her on). But if it isn't horrible, if all that is needed is a decision, just a small pure and painless step, then why resist? Perhaps it's like a dream. They say that she looked like she was sleeping, lying on her mattress covered with a plaid blanket, completely relaxed. A book was lying open on her breast. When her father opened the door the pages rustled. The only sound.

It's strange she got ready for bed. Three witnesses confirm this: she washed off her make-up, put on her nightgown, then presumably she read a little before falling asleep. Her hands slipped to her sides, the book flipped on to its spine and fell open. But she didn't close her eyes.

She forgot to close her eyes. That is what gave her away.

One enters death with open eyes.

But I was the one who had reached the minimum. You exist: everything else is extra, an illusion that might vanish at any moment and which you needn't believe in too much. I try to maintain peace of mind and distance, to deaden the feelings. I exist: I know it because of the body, functioning according to its established, independent, corporeal order. This requires a certain amount of effort. Only sometimes is the body Me, when the person and the reflection in the mirror overlap neatly. More often I quake before the untrustworthy, unknown object. The wall of skin retaining the layers of cells. I know that little shards of my insides threaten to pierce it at any moment. No. Why do I think my insides are jagged? Not shards, soft tentacles would emerge through the minute, evenly-spaced pores, like the arms of a starfish. That is how the second skin would look as it began to sprout and overgrow the first, covering it with moist feelers that would retract when touched. When touched, the skin would seem normal again.

Without love, one must endure existence without love for that pale skin, the pores, tufts of hair, callouses, the terror that washes over me when I look at it all: how is it possible, how is it possible that this is me? The mechanism, the exterior, a training ground for will and discipline only connected to consciousness by a slender thread.

This agility, this suspicious involvement in someone else's death. A sudden surge of treacherous energy. I restrain myself. I suppress laughter, stop myself from dancing with drunken abandon. From the outside it looks like sobbing. Her death threatens me, because it exposes my concealed longing.

I didn't know her. I know now that I didn't know her. That Wednesday afternoon she had come to say goodbye. I didn't understand. I didn't hear her. Three days later pain spread through my body like fire. I didn't know it was my heart. I thought that it was the accumulated horror that was exploding inside me.

How can I explain this to the anaesthetist? He says that

they'll give me a general.

As I lie on the high, narrow bed, the horror is loose again. I see Nina as she climbed into bed, covered herself and smoothed the blanket: then she looked around the room.

I look around the room and I know: this is how she felt. No one helped her get ready, she did it herself for long hours in her kitchen. A man would have done it differently. They would have found him with a bullet through his brain, slumped over a desk scattered with papers. The female death ritual is different. What did she do first? She sat at the kitchen table, took a piece of paper and a black felt tip pen and wrote in large printed letters: Danger – Gas! She stuck the note to the cupboard opposite her front door as a warning to those who would be first to enter. To avoid an explosion she removed the doorbell fuse: she wouldn't want anyone else to be hurt because of her.

When she first came home did she take off her green suit and put on her nightgown? Did she want to be a beautiful corpse? Then she left her underwear soaking. She didn't take it out, she just left it soaking in a washing-up bowl. Why didn't she wash it out? It was routine: she'd wash out the underwear tomorrow. Even when tomorrow would never come. As the water filled the washing-up bowl she must have known her tomorrow, when she could wash anything out, no longer existed. Does that indicate fear, hesitation? Does underwear left to soak say that she hoped that the phone might ring and that with her last ounce of strength she would lift the receiver? That someone at the other end would understand, hear the silent scream and get there in time? Maybe it is a sign that it is a hard step to take, even when the decision has been made, when the plan begins to unfold and this detail is all that exposes her unwillingness to yield. She unconsciously put off washing the underwear until 'tomorrow'. Longing still glowed in her, through the hands that turned off the water, took the washing-up bowl, put it down into the bathtub and left it there to stand. Two days later I came into the bathroom. It was still there.

Nina straightens up and looks into the mirror, that brief, sidelong glance, a quick check. In the mirror over the sink she saw a woman with light eyes and firmly-pressed lips, moving slowly, as if surprised, resting her hands on the smooth, cold porcelain. She leans forward and searches for something – a mark, a trace, an answer. She doesn't recognise the face. She stands before it as before a mask. Her being has already expanded to make room for death. The woman with the slightly familiar face is thirty-six years old and the decision slowly grows within her before her eyes. Energy returns. Yes, it will happen this evening, it is already happening. Recognising the warm tide the woman in the mirror sighs. She relaxes her tense shoulders.

When she turned out the light in the bathroom, did she cry?

She didn't have time. She had dishes to wash, books to arrange beside the bed that must go with her into her coffin, a letter to write to her parents.

'Please forgive me. Believe me this was the only way. For a long time now I haven't been alive.'

A few everyday words on a folded piece of paper, as if it

would be impolite to go without saying anything – but she didn't know what more there was to say. She could only hope that those who read it would see the handwriting as it slid down towards the right edge of the paper and the letters got smaller, illegible. She began with large, clear letters, big words. Maybe she really intended to explain. Then, from sentence to sentence, she achingly squeezed out the rest of the phrases, tired, already overwhelmed.

She sealed the locked kitchen door and windows with sticky tape from a wide brown roll. That must have taken a while. Being short she had to use a chair. Perhaps she got thirsty and reached for a glass of water. But the hand stopped in mid-air. No, she thought, what's the point?

I'd like to believe that she calmly drank a glass of water at that moment as she glanced once more round the kitchen. Is everything in order? She hated mess: scraps of food put away in the refrigerator, the table wiped. Sylvia Plath left her children breakfast set on the kitchen table before she shoved her head into the oven. Plates and cups draining on a red and white checked dish towel. She turns on the gas, picks up her book and lies down.

She left the door to the kitchen open.

She must have read only a few pages. Maybe she just watched and waited. The gas from the stove leaked out slowly. She waited until the book fell from her hand. She didn't close her eyes, the last she saw was the white of the wall, or already the white beyond the wall.

The white wall in front of the bed suddenly threatens me.

'No-oooo!'

It was a howl. Only now do I feel I must go all the way, that I must overcome this obstacle, too. All the accumulated horror that is choking me at this moment is no longer enough, it cannot be enough to stop me. I will write a letter to Natasha. Will she understand? On yellow paper I try to follow green lines. The letters dance before my eyes and I write blindly, not in my handwriting. I can't express this, the howl. No, that's not true: I don't dare. I hold it back, I want to protect her. We were driving from the sea coast to Zagreb. She slept in my arms, she was two years old. A blue vein was pulsing in her left cheek, peacefully, with the rhythm of sleep. But so visibly, on the surface, right under the skin, she was utterly vulnerable. I hid the place with my finger and with a movement of panic I covered her damp little head: everything is alright while she is with me, while I can firmly hold her close.

I looked at the yellow paper. In a long scraggly line I had written: 'Take care, take care, take care . . .' Because if I say what I'm thinking, that the yellow paper looks like the last piece of paper that I'll ever hold, snatching at that straw . . . I can't. One small part of my consciousness knows that this is all sentimental, unbearably sentimental, but I don't care. Lost, I look for an envelope, put the letter in it and dig around in my purse for something to show her how much I need her. Some tiny object that will travel with all those words for seven or ten days and arrive already devoid of meaning. In the meantime the thing will have taken place.

There is a picture card in my wallet, the kind you get with chocolate bars or bubble gum. I have no idea why it is there or what I've been saving it for. A small blue picture a little larger than a stamp, two panda bears hugging, dancing, or perhaps a little tipsy. One has a funny tilted red cap, the other a bow. Relieved, I slip the picture into the letter.

Now I can escape. Retreat inside, wrap rosy eyelids round self and shut out light, slip into deafness, pull into a closed core, turn into a pebble. Lie on my hip, pull my knees up to my chin and cover my head with the sheet. Breathe slowly, hibernating, freeze everything, absolutely everything, except a small firm dark spot, like a black hole, that the eye picks out somewhere on the distant inner horizon. Perhaps this is the end, where all colours meet, the focus of dispersion. Enter that hole and never re-emerge. That is how it will be. I will never completely re-emerge, that I know.

Behind my eyelids the colour of panic is crimson.

A momentary feeling of lack of air, the environment suddenly sucks me up. It is clear what is happening; the most complete conscious experience of void. Like fainting. Like an attack.

Longing very slowly penetrates from the body to the emptied brain, a clear feeing that I have *never* made peace with the illness. I have lied to myself until this very moment. Inside I see at once a brightly-lit image, a glittering crystal structure: all that sacrifice, asceticism, discipline, rejection, closing off and hoarding was not negation but longing. The entire system was functioning completely in reverse, like an inside out glove: there was no balance, no control. My great victory, the acceptance of death, was just a lie behind which lay a vast, indifferent greed. I cheated myself – or one part of me cheated another. Two parts, there are definitely two parts. What I believed to be the unique centre of my being – reason, peace, control – was a trick, a ploy to embrace the illness so that at the first opportunity I could take it by the throat and expel it from me. But I didn't know that. For six years I patiently built my mental framework, a secure construct in which I could manouevre safely, never let go, never relax, never grow attached to anyone, never trust, be rational. Only then could I overcome the fear of death which, no longer a fear, became the way I existed.

Though reduced to a mere presence, I want to *be*. I want to touch the firmness of objects with my hand. The wooden table in Ana's kitchen: look, this hand and table are one, I am in that wood, I feel it, there is nothing except me and the awareness of the hardness of that object, my presence in it, now. I want that presence, the night with Natasha's breath beside me. It is quiet, I am awake, I don't want to miss a single moment of her or my existence, our breathing, my greedy listening.

That possibility: to breathe, breathe, breathe.

Did anyone knock? Stop by and then go off, thinking Nina wasn't home? Did she reach for the phone? Why didn't she call anyone? She couldn't get out of herself, she couldn't go back, everything had already been set. Is there any difference between Nina and me at this moment? I see my body lying on the bed and a spasm surges from its depths and consumes it, slowly, from head to toe, a torrent that will stifle it, that shakes it. First the jaw, a phantom chattering distinctly heard in the quiet room, a strangely regular chattering, like the sound of a wooden toy, maybe a rattle. Then the entire body starts to shudder, slowly, stronger, rattling the bed. Something has grabbed it from within and is trying to get out.

Tears start to flow of themselves, I can't stop them. I can't scream. I can't lift my hands to cover my face with my palms. It is not me, this is no longer myself. There is no more bed, no room, no hallway, no hospital; just a shivering that has taken over and in which I'm completely lost.

But still, I'm breathing.

If I believed in God – if they'd taught me to believe – I could pray to him the way I saw my grandmother pray: she'd make a sign of the cross on her breast with her right hand, then bend her head, close her eyes and rest them on her folded hands. 'My good, my dear, my dearest Lord,' I'd whisper as to a lover, as to a child. 'You know that I've never prayed, because I didn't know that you existed . . .' My grandmother covered her head with a black scarf when she went to church. I stood in the doorway and she'd quickly sprinkle me with holy water from the font. She must have saved my soul by doing that, at least a little. And I'd also like to tell Him that I've no one left to turn to. Keep me alive. Please.

In summer we'd go off to an old house on an island. In the upstairs room that tall double bed that I would sink into at night and hear the cicadas and wake up from the light that fell on the pillow through the shutters, muted voices below and the smell of roasted coffee. Above the bed hung a picture of a woman, her hair flowing from one side of the frame to the other. The gilded frame held the thick hair to keep it from flying around the room. A pale face with raised eyes and gentle clasped hands that could hardly be seen through the hair, as through a shroud. 'She watches over you while you sleep,' my grandmother told me. Under her gaze I would slip peacefully into dreams.

I didn't know why grandmother often moved a string of black beads and a little silver cross through her fingers. Much later, when she was no longer alive and when the picture no longer hung on the wall, I learned that she was saying her rosary. She had a little prayer book bound in black leather in which she would put a picture of a saint at the place where her prayers had ended that day. The room was quiet, dark, full of mysterious furniture, huge black cabinets, a dressing table, a bureau. The shutters were never opened and narrow rays spread only on the floor. On the large bureau across from the bed where she kept her linen – a row of lavender, a row of stiff rustling sheets and pillow slips with lace edging – stood two plaster Madonnas. They were quite old even then, long faces, pink cheeks, slender noses from which paint was peeling and bright red lips, and they were gazing upwards too, hands clasped in prayer. The folds of their long white robes, the golden trim. Oh, how much easier it would be to believe in them, to pray to them, to entrust my sleep to them! But it is late. Grandmother is gone. The Madonnas are gone. They'll be coming for me soon, it's gone five o'clock.

There's still something I must do. I get up from the bed, take my purse and, with extreme caution, extract four objects that have absorbed power from other people. I am sure that a part of me is contained in them at this moment. Four objects of power. Thinking someone might come by I close the door to the room. First I take the little plastic mouse that Natasha gave me two years ago to protect me on my travels. She was afraid that she might lose me, the mother who might never come home, who simply might not wake up one morning. But travel seemed the most dangerous to her. The next object is an earring, the only one left of the pair that Nina gave me for my birthday. It is long, asymmetrical, some African nut painted gold. The paint has flaked away and tarnished since her death. I hold it firmly pressed in my right hand for a moment. The clasp of despair. Then I put it on the bed, by the mouse.

The third object I found in Athens. At nine o'clock in the evening all the stores in Plaka were closed, iron blinds were down, the narrow streets empty. I must find something for Natasha, I thought. I have to. Suddenly, as if my wish had made it happen, a patch of light, a store. I go in and see the earrings. I see only them and know that I've found them. The assistant packs them carefully, slips them into a cloth and then a box, as if he senses how precious they are. 'That's a phoenix,' Natasha said later. How that word rang in the ear! I had to take one of them with me. Maybe she sensed that I might need it. The bird glistens silver in a circle cast by the lamplight. Outside the circle are shadows and ghosts that live in this room. I can hear them dancing but I don't look up. My hands are in the light, arms bare to the elbow, fingers that slip from object to object with slow, caressing movements. The spirits are good.

The fourth object. Indecisively, as if compelled by necessity, a hand dips into the dark and comes out again, hiding something. No one must see it or touch it. 'This is for your health, you'll see that you will succeed,' Carmen said. She was quiet, she didn't know English well, she simply came up and gave it to me at the conference, looking around cautiously, as if confiding a secret. The act of giving made it magic. I kept touching it anxiously to check if it was there. I believed in it because of the way that she took me to the corner of the hall, an unknown woman who wanted to help me.

What power does this strange object from Mexico possess? A small paper picture (like the one that grandmother used to mark her place in the prayer book), with a glued-on copper horseshoe wound in red thread? On the picture inside the horseshoe is a rider on a horse, a warrior in armour and cape, with a helmet and plume. He holds a sword in his hand. The sea is behind him and mountains the same blue. A Spanish conquistador? A Roman soldier? On the ground a naked, bearded old man with one hand stretched out towards the rider, as if pleading for something. Who is the old man? Will the soldier strike him? On the back is a drawing of the sun, the comets and two half-moons. There is a cross in the middle with the words PODER Y VITA written horizontally and LUZ Y VERDAD vertically. I cover all four objects. Their power enters me. A timid lonely ritual before the void takes over – and I already hear the steps.

There is no more fear, just letting go.

Now I'll slip into sleep and that woman with the flowing hair, my grandmother's prayers, the old man with outstretched hand, the phoenix, the blushing plaster Madonna, all will watch over me. Once more grandmother will sprinkle water over my head and let me into the large, unlit hall. Down the end at the altar candles will glow. 'Kneel and don't be afraid,' she'll whisper, but I'll keep walking towards the light and the lilies. Now I see another painting and another cross: on the cross a man, a lot of gold and crimson and a strange fragrance that grows headier and headier. Almost at the flame, grandmother takes me by the hand and together, like in the story of the little match girl, we'll go up to heaven.

But the hall is full of light. Suddenly from the ceiling shine a hundred candles, a hundred silver light bulbs. Grandmother is gone and I hear a voice: 'Put out your arm and don't be afraid.' There are green tiles all around, an aquarium without water. I lie on a narrow table covered with a green blanket, they tie down my feet, the toreador anaesthetist gives me an oxygen mask.

'So you can breathe more easily.'

Oh, I know that you'll deceive me, but I don't mind.

Light as a feather, I'm glad as I grow lighter. There is no more burden, nothing is holding me down or hurting me anymore. Nothing can be changed. What a happy certainty! My left hand is already tied, the nurse ties down the right. She has a green cap, a green mask and glasses. I reach for her hand, I take it – and she firmly returns the clasp. At the same time fingers touch the right side of my neck. I can just hear a quiet, distant voice: 'Now be quiet. We have to make an important incision here.' No. No. I shake my head from left to right. The eyes are already closed, consciousness would like to resist, but all I can do is squeeze the hand

tighter. And that's the end.
The end.

2

I can't remember everything.

'Breathe, breathe.' An English voice penetrates the darkness in which I'm floating. I am not breathing.

Am I awake?

Am I alive?

I don't know. All I want is to stop the bits of consciousness spinning around and bumping into the edges of something dark and deep. The voice dips into a well – first clear, and then lost, as if tripping against obstacles on its way down. It mixes with other sounds, with the sound of blood swirling in giddy circles, faster and faster. Terrified I try to suck in air, catch it with my open mouth, but something is inside, something is inside. It is smothering me, I have to retch it out. They are pulling out a long tube with a sudden jerk from my throat, tearing the membranes. A deep sigh. Then a sharp pain under my stomach cuts me in half.

'Your kidney is functioning.'

I can hear. I understand. I don't understand. It means nothing to me. My motionless tongue lies dry and swollen like a chunk of wood. I want to say something. I want to say it hurts. Nothing exists but this flaming pain that won't let me breathe. I cough up long strings of phlegm from my lungs. They are balled up down at the very bottom, near the incision. If I stretch out, the incision will snap. It will gape like a huge red mouth. Voices by the head of the bed. Hands attach a mask to my nose: suddenly it seems as if I'm in a meadow, a cool breeze caressing my face. A light rain is falling and I take long, light steps . . .

Nausea. Coughing. The incision burns me.

'Lay still.' A cool hand touches my forehead but nausea climbs up from the stomach, swells, advances. I turn my head to the side. A stream of something lukewarm and sticky spurts in a convulsion. At the same time a sharp stab in the neck where a slender tube enters the vein. I'm hot, then colder and colder.

Wake up, I say to myself, you've got to wake up.

A needle is in my left arm above the elbow. Something cold is flowing through it that stings. My right arm looks free and I slowly lift my hand and place it on my stomach. Cautiously I probe the long wound with a finger. In a slow, circular motion I move my palm over my skin. The agitated, swollen fingertips inch across the body then the bed: hot, moist, rough, dry – skin, cloth, cold bars. Further and the fingers drop into empty space, the void. Where the incision stops a tube juts from the stomach, attached with sticking plaster to the outside of my thigh. There is another tube that chafes between my legs. I don't dare to move for fear something will drop out, my guts will fall out. I absorb sounds. With effort I dive through an ocean of sounds. I try to discern my own breathing: it is someone else's breathing, heavy, strained, as if a mountain were breathing. Wheezing. The scraping of shoes. The distant ring of a telephone. Sounds multiply and grow, the roaring slaps me like ocean waves. One shoe becomes many, the telephone is ringing constantly.

Quite near, something made of glass rattles in a metal dish.

The ping hits me like lightning, so bright that it hurts. Then hushed voices fill the space above me. They filter down, covering me, smothering, they come closer. The fidgety squeaking of rubber soles on linoleum. They are discussing my heart. Again! Warmth from the wound rises diagonally towards my chest. I recognise that heat, the hesitation, a muffled pounding and then silence between two irregular, uncertain beats. Say something, explain to them . . . I compose a whole sentence in my head, piece it together bit by bit. I can clearly see the words and letters. I repeat them in my head, but the sound does not come out. My throat is full of sand. Who cares.

Suddenly I seem so heavy that I drift off to sleep.

'Water.' I think that was my whisper.

They put a sponge soaked in ice water in my mouth. 'More.'

I suck tiny sips, drink it up with my whole body as if I'm taking a bath. Here I am, on the surface again. Disintegration is behind me, past. Now I will be able to drink, gulp down a full pitcher of water or tea. I can already think about tea. I'll sit in Jelena's kitchen, at the table covered by the dark blue tablecloth with tiny white lilies. A silver teapot will stand on it. I will take a cup and pour. The first sips will be quite small and cautious. It will swill round my mouth and slip slowly down my throat. Then suddenly I'll greedily swallow the rest. I'll drink until I've emptied the pot, until I am so full of liquid that it disgusts me.

My mouth is bitter with disgust, as if I've already had the tea.

Someone is gently adjusting the pillow under my head.

'My name is Joanne.'

I open my eyes and through water I see Nina. She is leaning over me. 'Everything is alright,' she says. Serenity fills me. I recognise the familiar lines of her face, the blonde hair cut straight above the forehead, the thin stern lips, the penetrating eyes.

'You've come back,' I say, and try to smile.

She is silent now. She watches me, worried.

'Don't you recognise me?' I ask, lifting my hand towards her.

'Be calm,' she says. 'You mustn't move.'

Gradually I become suspicious. Where am I? In the middle of a huge brightly-lit room crowded with people, beds, machines. I recognise the doctor. The pain I feel is real. Is this the hospital? I am not sure. I don't see a single window. Perhaps I'm underground. This may be a dream, or an image built by my fear. Nina is saying something and gently rubbing my forehead. It's been six months since she was buried. When I turn round perhaps her back will be blank, like a figure cut out of cardboard. Just empty whiteness. I must touch her hand: it is warm.

The touch makes me shiver.

The doctor comes up and says that I have to sleep. But I mustn't. When I wake up I won't know where I am.

My body lies naked under a thin blanket. When I was seven or eight years old, in the evening, in bed, I imagined that my body was lighter than air. Every night I'd go off on long trips. On the way back it would become heavy and pull me to the ground. Now I long to feel that weight, to become conscious of every joint, my knees, my fingers, my lungs, my stomach.

I have small breasts and wide hips, narrow shoulders, a long, thin face. My spine is twisted so that the tips of the ribs on my left side stick out visibly. On my right hand the veins are swollen, there are scars from needles, places where the skin is paper thin. I'm short-sighted. When I look in the mirror, I like only some parts. The full, slightly-crooked mouth. The large white teeth that sometimes gleam. The joints on the hands and feet with slender, articulated bones – they look fragile. I don't like the rest: a little fat on the stomach, stretch lines, cellulite, rough skin on the elbows and heels, the skin on my face that is quickly ageing.

Nonetheless, I long for it, the pain that reduces me to a body. Have I finally admitted to myself that I want it?

I am in another bed, another room. An unfamiliar woman's face is leaning over me, quite close. A lock of her dark hair blocks my view. With a measured, abrupt movement she pulls a long tube out of my neck. Then she inserts a new one. I feel a slight uneasiness deep inside. If I make the slightest move, if her hand trembles, the tip might

46

pierce the wall of the artery. I'd feel pain that would take my breath away, but it would be too late. On the outside nothing would be visible until my lips suddenly turned blue.

'Does it hurt?'

Her breath on my face.

'No, no. It doesn't hurt.' But she appeared so unexpectedly. Shaking with effort, I press my stomach firmly with my hands. 'It's done,' she says. Expanding, my scream fills every corner of the room.

The chronological order of events escapes me, whole days are missing. They stretch like grey, thick spots on a wall, nothing legible underneath. In the window there are red azaleas. Is it day or night? The telephone rings. 'Yes, yes. I'm fine.' Who was it? The thread of memory is sliced into fragments by the light, abruptly, repeatedly turning on and off. I can't establish order.

Sleep, just sleep.

How long have I been here? How long has this been going on? From time to time I open my eyes. Then I close them, but do not drift asleep. I'm jerked from napping by sounds in the hallway and that voice. Inside me something whispers: 'Watch out, don't fall asleep.' I see horrible black water and slowly wade into it, up to my waist, up to my neck, until I no longer feel my body. I am calm because I am sure that I know how to swim. I want to take a stroke with my arms, but they do not obey me because they are not mine at all. You should have thought of that before, I tell myself. The alien arms make panicked, drowning motions. I sit pressed into my mind. I crouch rigid with fear and watch the body submerging, the black liquid seeping into my mouth. 'I can't breathe. I can't breathe.' Then a long, drawn-out moan as water swallows everything and I can no longer see.

The nurse thinks I am moaning from pain and she gives me a shot which leaves me quiet for a while, groggy, on the verge of consciousness. Then the struggle begins again, the wading into water repeated like a scene from a film that must be practised until perfect. Just as I catch myself on the edge of sleep, on the edge of drowning (what part of me is waiting for that moment?), violent cramps suddenly shoot through my arms and legs. Balls are rolling through my muscles, I watch how they lift the taut skin, convulse and relax. My fingers grow rigid, the pain wakes me up. I know what that means: 'Swim, swim, swim!' I swim. But I always drown in the end, exhausted from the effort of keeping myself afloat. When the water stops rippling over my head, I open my eyes, completely drenched, in the dark, where I can't see a thing.

Whenever I woke I felt chilled, as if I was in a draught. Whenever I open my eyes it seems as if I am somewhere new. I can't follow the changes: they set up another bed next to mine; tulips and an orchid in a vase appeared in the window next to the azaleas. Disturbing. I have to be careful where I look: from time to time a bright blueness floods the room and each thing seems so visible that my head aches.

When I saw Grace I didn't recognise her right away. She stood for a moment in the middle of the room, her coat buttoned to the neck.

'It's snowing outside,' she said.

'Snow?' I repeated surprised. 'Outside?'

The word hung somehow uncertainly in the dusk, as if I was hearing it for the first time and listening carefully to its new sound.

Grace had come up from New York. 'Outside' was the train, the dry squeak of snow on the street, her coat, the way she rubbed her hands. When I touched her her skin was still icy. 'Outside' is waiting for me. It hadn't occurred to me for a while that it existed, that things happened out there, that snow could be falling. I was so totally enclosed that I asked myself if I would ever get out. Outside had no meaning, I couldn't reach it. I could go no further than the edge of the bed – the void – then the wall, that I can't reach, can't touch. Perhaps it is an illusion. It's safer to close my eyes. I didn't know what to do with 'snow' in the room, with the word 'snow', the way Grace had said it. 'Snow' and 'outside' belonged to the same frightening category as 'future'.

Grace sits, uncertain, at the head of my bed. Just then her familiar face turns into a bridge from before to after, outside to inside, and it is quite easy for me to shift into the future, or at least I think that is what I am doing. This, now, here, the hospital – all ceases to exist. I am in it by chance. It is merely a short, meaningless interval that cannot disturb my life. I sit up in bed – see, I can sit up in bed! – and finally I can speak. Instead of telling her about the fear, about how sorry I was that I didn't let her come with me that evening, how I'd wanted to call her. I talk

about books and travel as if I've forgotten the past with unbelievable speed. But I can't completely fool myself. As I
watch her, as I speak, I envy her. The ease with which she
pulled up the chair and sat down. The way she leans back,
crossing her legs, resting her chin on her elbow. The way
she gets up and goes to the door, opens it, washes her
hands and fills a glass with water.

She stands in the frame of light, her head tossed back a
bit, sipping, looking at me over the rim, as if this were the
most natural thing in the world to do, to lean against the
doorframe and absentmindedly sip a glass of water.

On the axis of time, snow was located unbelievably far
away.

Then she picks up her crumpled woven leather purse
and takes out an open pack of peppermint candies, some
paper handkerchiefs, a ballpoint pen, a bottle of face lotion,
a notebook: in case they come in handy. Things that happen to be in her purse. I don't know where to start. I can't
eat, or blow my nose, or write. The face lotion, lost on the
night table, looks utterly meaningless. Cosmetics! But the
clumsy rummaging around in her purse, the gesture . . .
With one hand she lifts up my head and with the other she
brought the glass to my lips.

Had I already talked to her about my mother?

I have nothing belonging to my mother except photographs, memories on photographs, and I don't even have
those with me. Whenever we meet, we are long and pain-
fully silent. We no longer even gossip about father. That
would be a sign of intimacy, familiarity. The longing is hidden in quick, exploratory glances (she thinks that I don't

notice them), the motions of hands that smooth invisible wrinkles on the edge of the tablecloth, unfinished sentences. 'How are you?' A formula for two women who have forgotten their common language to communicate, after so many years have passed. 'Fine.' My unconvincing answer means forget it, enough, let's not get into that. Let's not get into ourselves.

Her guilt, my guilt, words that cannot be spoken. What is our language if not those mute gestures of recognition in the presence of others, always in the presence of others (father, brother)? Whenever we end up alone the words clot and the gestures come of themselves, empty, hollow, meaningless.

Maybe still there is touch.

Grace combs me, carefully pulling the comb through my hair. The tangled parts she frees with her fingers.

First mother would touch my forehead with her hand. Then, propped up with pillows, she would wrap a cold compress on my forehead, then bring in strong, fragrant linden tea brewed in a pot decorated with red ladybugs. I would stir the tea for a long time with a spoon, for as long as she sits on the edge of the bed next to me. Now and then she would touch my hair, lifting locks from my forehead as if afraid to show tenderness. I can't remember other times that she touched me. But they must have been there: the hands that washed my hair, led me across the street, hugged me close. Why can't I remember them?

Later, the unnameable between us.

But I am still little, there is nothing unnameable yet. I am little, lonely and sick and she will come and hug me and then . . .

No. She won't come.

'How I wish my mother was here,' I say.

'I know,' Grace says. She puts down the comb and ties my hair in a ponytail with a rubber band.

Mother was cold, beautiful and self-absorbed.

On the wedding photograph she wears a felt hat with net and a string of pearls around her neck. The raised veil shows her perfectly symmetrical face and thick, lightly-waved brown hair that fell in curls to the sides. She is twenty-one. She looks straight at the camera and smiles. Is my memory playing tricks or was she wearing lipstick? That was 1949. How did she get hold of lipstick? At school they taught us how the enemy burnt villages and devastated cities, leaving a ravaged landscape behind them. I imagined smoking ruins, brigades of people cleaning the streets cluttered with tiles, rafters and bits of furniture, dressed in miserable rags and remnants of uniforms. Barefoot, thin and hungry, like in the cinema newsreel showing scenes of 'renovation and rebuilding'. Food was bought with coupons. There were no clothes in the stores. There were no private shops. No fashion salons with little hats for fashionable young women who were no longer interested in the war.

There must have been such a store, though, even during the war itself – hats, artificial flowers, black, elbow-length gloves, lace collars, plisse, mother of pearl buttons. It can't all have been like what we learned in school. But she didn't talk about that. No one spoke about the war, as if it were something that ought to be erased.

Seven or eight years later she is on a beach. Again she has
a hat, this time made of straw. Her lips are made up even
more. Revolutionary puritanism is on the wane. She is
stretched out in a blue, two-piece bathing suit. I remember
that it was blue even though the photograph is in black and
white. It wasn't a real bikini, but nonetheless . . . I am
somewhere nearby. I watch her as she leans back on her
right hand, cocks her head, smiles. How beautiful she is,
tanned, firm! The hat is Italian and the bathing suit is too.
That summer – yes it was that summer – she went to visit
her aunt. The first trip abroad. (Italy was no longer the
occupying force that one should hate and she spoke Italian.
During the occupation she was courted by Italian soldiers.)
Luxurious department stores. Morning espresso in a café.
High-heeled sandals with thin straps that gently wrap
around the ankles. Fingernail polish, wonderful-smelling
soap. Perfume.

She came back by boat. Waiting on the shore were my
father, two children, a two-room apartment, a job, cooking,
laundry by hand, Sunday strolls, New Year celebrations,
summer dancing on the Army Club terrace. Perhaps she
thought: 'It's too late, I can't change anything any more.'

Irredeemably, she leaves the boat.

The nurse brought lunch. Grace mashed the potatoes
with a fork. She cut the meat up into little bits then put
them in my mouth with a spoon.

Mama, the unknown woman, sits opposite me. We are
eating lunch. How is the soup?

'Fine.'

'I made it the way you like it.'

53

'I know, mama, the soup is good. You put my favourite noodles in it.'

But the soup is not food, it is a vehicle through which we communicate. She tries to make contact through food, I keep insisting on words. I want to extract her innermost self in speech. I no longer accept the mutely physical: eat, eat. Potatoes, fish, salad, peas, freshly-baked bread, crêpes, macaroni, red wine – their secret meaning. Some elaborate dish is on my plate that she has been preparing all morning and I can hardly taste it. If I don't eat it, if I don't clear my plate, it will make her sad. She had a terrible time getting hold of this wonderful piece of meat. So tender. A shame to waste it. So I eat because I feel guilty. I accept the emotions hidden in the meat: spices, fragrances, the magic of the pot, the set table, the full plate. Not yet daring to get up from the table I stuff the food into my stomach, letting her know in her language that I understand the message, to satisfy her and slightly diminish my guilt. This is the only way to grab a little of her love for me.

There must have been some other language between us at some time. She taught me to name objects and utter words, murmuring lovingly to me. I remember I used to cry in that language. I couldn't bear to be separated from her for even a moment. How could she forget that? When she speaks of me today, she only remembers my earliest years. She cannot even speak of when I started school. I find it hard to say her name out loud. It sounds strange. What has happened to us? I'd ask her, if I only knew how, if I could be sure she'd answer. She was already afraid of words back then, didn't trust them, wasn't sure of their meaning. I must unravel her through signs, through memory and photographs, old ball gowns, handiwork and brief phone conversations, like reading coffee grounds. Or as if she was no longer alive.

'Don't go,' I tell Grace. 'Stay a little longer.' With slow movements she puts on her coat, which has grown heavier in the meantime. She leaves. She comes back. She says that she will come again.

For a moment it feels as if my insides are made of glass, a sphere covered with tiny mirrors, like in a disco, turning and flicking beams of white light across the dancers. But the mirrors face inwards, reflecting into one another, making a multiplied symmetrical crystal structure without end, or its end is out of sight. Thoughts, feelings, events, illuminated by the miniature shafts of light, are reflected by each mirror and join in a network of memory where even the tiniest instant of the past is never lost.

A sense of being physically split in two comes over me. I feel an unbearable tension and then a crack. The crack widens. I break like a thin, brittle piece of paper. I crumble, fluttering around the room. The nightmare Me slips into a world of blurred images and hallucination. Then it erupts from the depths, dark, wild, unpredictable. It shakes me, it won't let go. It pulls down, bites my stomach, rips off chunks of flesh, perforates. I can do nothing against it. High above, someone is watching it all. That is also me. I perspire and lose consciousness breathing the sweet smell of my own sweat.

At night the room grows smaller. The ceiling descends

slowly, a few centimetres at a time. Now it's within reach I can discern details, the colour and structure of the plastic squares, the seams where they connect, the little and big holes in the surface. They seem to move. Are they pores through which the ceiling is breathing? It's getting dark as if a storm is brewing. The room is shrinking, the walls pressing close to one another. I lie in a long, narrow space. The ceiling is straight above me. I see the pores, as large as a fish's gills. They pulsate. The ceiling is breathing. The pores are soaking up the air, wrenching it from my mouth. There's less and less air. It's hard to breathe. I turn my head but the ceiling continues to descend and the walls get closer. I spread out my hands to stop the walls falling on me, but I have no way of propping up the ceiling. If I fall asleep it will all cave in on me. I must not sleep. No. No.

Finally a little light. The walls slip back and grow larger. This is no longer a room, it is a great hall and the light comes from narrow windows near the top. My eyes grow accustomed to the brown semi-dark. It is cold. The room is freezing and people are squatting crouched along the walls, only a few of them are standing up. They all wear thin hospital nightshirts, open at the back. I see the staring eyes and flapping hands, mouths moving soundlessly, silent, stiff, like a silent movie. Maniacs. The hall is part of an asylum. I am among lunatics, I can see it in their eyes. I feel my way around but there are no doors anywhere. No one pays any attention. I go from one to another, I want to ask something. My voice swells in my mouth and dies. Not even I can step outside myself. I have to bury all that horror inside and stay silent. Silent. Suddenly I realise that they don't care whether the room has doors or not, they wouldn't be able to leave anyway. Their mouths are stuffed with lead. That lead in their mouths – I can still taste it.

People keep going in and out. Two nurses turn my heavy body, they change the sheets. The doctors measure my pulse, uncover my belly, feel it, part my eyelids. Doctor Weiss takes off his glasses and nods his head. He leans over, takes the plastic urine sack attached to my body and holds it high in the air. The kidney is functioning. The urine is dark with blood.

'See that!' he says joyously. 'That's great!'

I don't dare get excited and smile feebly, still so weak that I shiver with foreboding at the word 'great'. Left alone I cry long and quietly. I think 'good, the fear will drain out of me'.

'Do you remember you had a visitor?' the nurse asks as she replaces the intravenous needle. She must be thinking of Grace. But she says that Grace came a few days ago. She says I had a visitor this afternoon too.

I know that they came. Above my head a bedside lamp glowed. It was quiet in the semi-darkness of the room, I didn't hear any steps. First Jelena came in wearing a blue ski jacket. Her face was indistinct in the gloom, but I could see the blue jacket glisten. She stood at the foot of the bed and watched me, concerned, sad. Then the room began to fill up: Mira came in, Grace appeared again, Ana, Hana, my mother, Natasha. It was getting crowded. Some had to stand at the doorway, I could only just make them out. They looked at me, all women's faces – and on them I

57

could see that I'm wrong even now for remaining silent. I didn't know what to say. I am afraid they expected more from me, a sudden spurt of exuberance, perhaps. Obvious signs of a transformation. For me to say, at least now: 'Everything is all right. Go home. I'm so tired. I'll be happy tomorrow, when tomorrow comes. We'll laugh together at my fear, my silliness. We'll get drunk and I will wonder, half drunk: "Good Lord, is it possible? Was I really in that hospital?" Winter will just have passed, it will be far away. You will be my valuable witnesses, without you I wouldn't be certain. Pain is forgotten so easily.' But I can't say it. Not now.

Maybe they think I'm asleep. No matter what they try to tell me, all together like that, I won't hear them, feel their breath, smell them. They were on the other side. There was a sheet of glass between us that I could touch and even taste with my tongue. But I can't open it like a window. I shouted out loud: 'I can't!' I heard myself distinctly, re-peating 'I can't!' pressed up against the glassy surface. But the taste of lead wouldn't go away and I realised that only I could hear my voice. They couldn't hear me with that cold, transparent thing between us. They could only see my lips opening, my hands waving in the distance, a woman in a hospital nightshirt whose mute face they could hardly recognise.

When they left, I dreamt of walking down a street. I hear a thud. I turn around and see a dog, a large German shepherd. I'm not sure what has happened. Has a car hit it or has someone chopped off his right hind leg with an axe? The dog is lying on its side. A black hole gapes on its haunch, around it clotted blood. I have a terrible need to inspect the hole but I don't dare. I just stand there, over the dog. I ask myself whether there is any point in keeping it alive when it can't survive on three legs. The dog's life or death hangs on my decision. I know that, but still I avert my eyes from the wound. I don't know whether I saved him or not. When I woke up I felt sick. I thought: 'I should have saved him. I was afraid of getting dirty. There was blood everywhere.'

'It's not a good sign to dream blood.' My mother's words.

But I can't fend off dreams. Again I dream of blood, even more blood. I am standing in a dark room, light from the corridor filtering in through the open door. A room I know quite well, so well that even in the half-light I recognise the dialysis machine, tall somehow, narrow, twice its usual size. It looks remarkably like a hot-water boiler, the kind you used to see in old-fashioned bathrooms. I know that it's a dialysis machine and not a boiler, even though there is a large bathtub right next to it. A thick rubber tube runs through the bathtub, a transparent garden hose. I am on dialysis and the rubber hose connects the machine to my left arm. Pale light filters into the room from the corridor. Dimly I see my blood flowing through the hose. Suddenly the electricity shuts down. I am petrified. I hear someone is coming. Relief! Those are my mother's footsteps.

'Turn off the pump, turn off the pump! My blood is going to spill out all over the place!' I scream with all my might.

Mother is confused, she can't figure out what to do. She

gropes for a light switch in the corridor. She can't find it but neither will she come into the dark room and stays standing in the lighted corridor, as if frightened. The hose has already snapped. Blood is spurting and filling the bathtub in a gushing stream. With my own hand I grab one end of the hose, hold it high above the bathtub, firmly gripping the ends. The light from the corridor illuminates the blood through the transparent hose. It is not dark and thick, but light and thin, as if mixed with water. I feel myself growing limp. I won't be able to hold this position much longer. Already frantic I shout to mother, still standing there: 'Don't let the blood spill out! That is my blood! It will spill out, spill out ...' I watch her helplessly. Pointing to the hose with the cloudy pink liquid, she starts to laugh. 'That's not blood. That's not blood at all,' she says and the loud laughter echoes round the room.

I must have started crying in the middle of the dream for when I opened my eyes my cheeks were already wet. The telephone woke me. I heard her voice. Really her, her voice, coming from afar, finally.

I trembled.

I remember that day well, that early morning. Sounds from the hallway, my moist hands, pale bands of sunlight on the curtain, the smell of coffee.

I'll tell her that I'm having a hard time, I thought, that images of dying dogs are haunting me, that I saw a bathtub full of blood. I'll tell her that I feel as if they've peeled away my skin and that I still hear the echo of that laughter from the dream. I'll tell her the dream. Maybe she'll recall the scene in the bathroom.

I was seventeen. The bathroom was opposite my room across the hall, so dark that the lamp had to be on all day. On the left was a bathtub and on the right a tall, wood-fired hot-water boiler, just like in the dream. That evening I told her – it was summertime, the light was on in the bathroom – that I was leaving home. She said: 'Don't.' She didn't say don't. She stood to one side, her arms hanging helplessly, and let me go. She didn't say anything to father, she didn't have to tell father anything. He knew.

Not long afterwards I slit both my wrists. An attempted suicide. The shirt was drenched with blood. I stood in a stuffy phone booth, both hands bandaged, and told her I'd tried to kill myself. She didn't fully understand. The line was bad. Several other people were waiting, already impatient. One plump young man with stains of perspiration under his arms came too close to the door, almost leaned on it. I couldn't shout or explain. I repeated the words once more: 'I slit my wrists.' The words sounded unconvincing in the booth, unreal. An aborted suicide: it sounded like a failure. I was ashamed of my failure. Finally she understood.

'Do you want me to come?' she asked.

Did I want her to come? She expected me to decide instead of her. But I couldn't, I couldn't tell her that I wanted her to. The fact that she had asked interfered. She should have known that you do not ask. The question devastates.

No, I won't tell her anything. Just that I'm fine, that the operation was a success. I won't mention the dog or the blood. I won't even think about it.

I don't dare mention all that. She will become even more alien to me, grow completely distant. I don't feel ready to be left without her, without her strange love. I must leave myself that option open. Perhaps she'll come – or at least write a letter in which she'll explain why, addressing me, she slips and uses my brother's name instead of mine.

I love her photographs. It seems that I can only understand her through them. The life that she has never discussed – before me, my brother, father – as if it never existed. It's hard to believe that she was that little blonde girl obediently sitting on a chair, holding a doll in her hand. She was a child, then a young woman with a golden necklace from which a medallion hung. Wearing a silk dress with padded shoulders she seemed confident, even haughty. Her left hand resting on her hip; long, flowing hair. In lively, fresh handwriting on the back of the picture it says: 'A memento to my dear friend Mira – 4/21/43.' Whatever can have happened to her friend Mira since that day and is that the same person in another picture sitting on a wall, in profile, while my mother contemplates the sea with her hands in her pockets? Does she still remember her? What does she remember? Or did she have to forget, time and time again, in order to get by?

When I am near her, in the same house, I get nervous. I can't do anything. I drift from room to kitchen. She won't let me help her. I sit at the table with nothing to do, redundant. I don't know where to put my hands. She expects me to tell her about my life, but I would rather peel potatoes, chop onions and mix batter. Back in my room I lie there reading a book. I have no peace of mind. My conscience bothers me. I'm trying but I am not with her. Days, years pass in trying.

But what does it mean, after all, 'to be with her'? I could only really be with her when she wasn't there. Her absence, my sense of desertion, that is what brings us close.

No – I won't say anything to her.

I tell her that the operation has been a success, that she needn't worry. She asks if I need anything. No. Am I sure? Yes. Do I want her to come? 'No, mama, no. It's too late.'

Droplets run down the receiver, like a windowpane.

Get out of bed, but it's not so simple: the intravenous tubes, catheters, plastic bags, inputs and outputs – one must not disturb their order. There is a set procedure for getting up: the bed is motorised; first tilt into a sitting position by pressing a button. Lower the legs, first one then the other, manhandling them into slippers. Cautiously, without bending over, or the pain will become blinding. Now I am on the edge. A mobile stand awaits me – hooks above, wheels below. The tubes, bags and catheters must be hung from its hooks or attached to its bars with adhesive tape, so that they don't get in the way as I walk. I get up by grabbing a bar with my right hand and pushing off the bed with my left. The whole process is so complicated and exhausting that it is impossible to simply give up and lie back down once I'm on my feet. Standing, every inch of my body resists separately. I can't feel my legs, just the way they tremble. There is nothing that I can really rely on. My entire upper body is completely unnecessary, pressing on the incision that already drags downward, towards the ground. My heart pounds faster, I'm short of breath. My hands feebly grip the slippery bar. A mass of uncoordinated parts tentatively wobbles, shudders, pants, slips, stumbles, drips, lurches frantically and seems as if any second it will crash to the floor. But it doesn't.

While I stand catching my breath, it seems as if I've lost, at least briefly, the presence of the other part, the split that agonises me while I'm lying down. There is no mind coldly observing from its own centre as the body flounders. All the great quivering heap wants is to get up, walk, fall, rise, crawl, be. The brain serves only to concentrate on the first step. The eyes keep watch for obstacles while, stumbling, I succeed in pushing the bar over the threshold of the room. I walk. I must keep my balance. I mustn't trip. I must hold the bar with one hand and my belly with the other and step slowly, one foot in front of the other.

I see a long, smooth corridor in front of me, like a tunnel lit with yellow lights. At the end in the far distance I can just barely make out a door. Or at least I think I can make it out, because I know that there must be a door there – this effort would be pointless if there were no exit at the end of the tunnel. But I have no strength to imagine what might be beyond and even the glance into the distance makes me dizzy and exhausted. I have never been forced to think of every single inch to be traversed, all the traps that lie in the polished linoleum, the handbar that turns down there into a slender thread – a guideline – the obstacles on the way that must be avoided: scales, a bicycle, a waste basket, the food trolley, a table with medicines, the door that is open or might suddenly swing open. A discouraging quantity of objects and people that I might bump into.

I look ahead, sense the space still to be conquered. If I thought about it, I'd give up instantly: there must be a door at the end of the corridor, and stairs beyond it, then a turn, then a long corridor, a door, the street, another street, the city. This city, another city. Buildings, rooms, stairs, elevators, cars, subways, airplanes – it is impossible to master, even to imagine. I'm short of time. I can grasp it for no more than a moment. I can only understand tiny segments, microscopic particles. I cannot distinguish the s quence of days and nights or mornings and afternoons. Only a moment when I opened my eyes and saw the nurse's temple, tiny light hairs at the end of her eyebrow, a moment when something scratched in my throat or a door squeaked. The rhythm takes hold and then it's gone again and leaves me to make my way utterly alone in an inner space with no way to orient myself. When I leave that space I have no sense of how much time has passed.

I creep along the wall, pulling along my feet in their plastic clogs. I hear the dry, squeaky sliding of their soles as I walk along the path of fresh untrampled snow. Seven, eight steps, then turn and back. I am alrea ly so exhausted – perhaps I might have a glass of water? I'll go down to the bathroom, I'll pour it myself, then I'll lean on the doorframe . . . Lost in thought, absentmindedly sipping the glass of water. I can't remember when I last did that, without a care. Years. It took some time to break the habit. Now I feel as if I could.

I dreamt about water, especially in the summer lying in hospital in Zagreb. My room faces west. The blinds are broken and can't be closed. The air conditioning hasn't worked for ages. My mattress is wrapped in nylon which is never taken off, even in summertime. A thin sheet is pulled over it. You lie there for hours in blinding light, in a room without a breath of fresh air, your back glued to the sheet. The damp stain of perspiration slowly spreads, like an island floating in a white ocean. The body lies on the island. Perspiration runs down the temples, drips into the eyes, into the mouth. It streams down the neck, between the breasts, before dribbling severally off the stomach. Drops slowly slide round the waist.

I am thirsty. My lips are peeling they are so dry. I lick the sweat from my upper lip: my tongue is so thickly coated that it sticks to the roof of my mouth. I suck spit, but none is left. I must have some water, at least a little.

The nurses in Zagreb offer me a plastic cup of lukewarm, sweetish water (I wouldn't want cold water, it lures you to drink more). 'Only a sip now!' they say. Yes, I'll just rinse out my mouth, get rid of the salty taste of thirst in my throat. I won't drink. I know that I must not drink. First I'll hold the cup for a bit in my hand, I won't drink it all at once, though I'd like to. It's an exercise. Then I'll sniff it. Water smells like damp plants, like a cellar. With a ritual movement I'll moisten my lips and tongue. The first sip will be very small, a cautious test. I'll take the second sip in my mouth as if I'm eating, like a bit of apple, and then I'll chew it slowly, chop it up, make it into mush that I can swallow as slowly as possible. For a long time its taste will be mixed with spit. Until in the end all that is left is spit. Until that dries up too.

Thirst is hard for me to bear. Water is my obsession. It

obsesses me like an enemy. It has a physical presence, supple, gleaming, perfectly transparent. I see it everywhere: in faucets, in the droplets of the shower, in the pot for soup, in wine, in milk, in the sea. You have to be on your guard, always on your guard. Water is a small death, a mute, seductive suppleness. The glass should be filled only half way, never to the rim. You must be sly in your approach to anything liquid. Never preoccupied. Never absentminded. Don't finish anything. Don't drink suddenly. Be aware of the danger and keep it under control. Don't submit to the simple pleasure of quenching your thirst with a glass of water.

I know a girl in Paris who has been on dialysis for fourteen years. She has a miniature fountain on a table at home. When she is thirsty she turns it on and watches the water. Sitting in her apartment on rue des Ecoles. It is summer, the afternoon is close, the blinds are down. The air conditioning is on but she can still hardly breathe. She perspires and greedily watches the water. A grim helplessness.

My father doesn't drink because he would never be able to stop. He eats ice. He scoops up a spoonful of crushed ice and then chews it long and loud at the table. Sometimes he delights in freezing wine mixed with water as a special treat.

I go into the bathroom, turn on the tap and lean against the wall, letting it run. I stare at the straight stream the way she looks at her fountain, as it runs down the plughole at the bottom of the white washbasin and my mouth is completely dry. My tongue parched. When the tap is covered with beads of water from the cold, I take a paper cup the colour of sand with a design of tiny brown leaves from the shelf and fill it to the brim. On purpose. There, that's it.

Now I will drink, drink, drink. One cup. Two. And then I'll stop counting. I'll drink fruit juices. Orange juice from tall slender glasses, with a straw and lots of ice. Dark berry juice that turns your tongue blue. Thick strawberry juice, real lemonade that you have to stir for ages with a spoon to melt the sugar at the bottom. Beer without foam, Coca-Cola with a slice of lemon, Schweppes, milk from the refrigerator, mineral water, red wine. I'll have *café au lait* for breakfast in the morning, Earl Grey tea in the afternoon, then coffee with whipped cream. When I wake up at night from thirst – dreaming I was drinking the sea – I'll pour myself a glass of water in the dark, drink it down with closed eyes and go back to bed. I won't even really wake up.

My teeth went numb at the first sip. I gulped twice, abruptly, as if ridding myself of something unpleasant. I couldn't go on.

Not too fast, not too fast!

The cup was still half full.

Drink it. I brought the cup to my lips. You must! When I took the next gulp, my stomach convulsed and I thought I might vomit. Fear. I crumpled the cup, clutched the washbasin and burst into tears. The tears dribbled down that same drain with the water. Tears. Water. Tears. Water.

What good was it all if I can't drink water, if I don't allow myself to drink my fill?

I can at least splash my face. Submerge my face in handfuls of cold water. That much I can do. I hold my cupped hands quite close to my eyes and look up. Someone else is splashing my face. I am standing bent over above a washbasin and someone else's hands are bringing water to my face. I feel the movement, the moisture drying on my skin and pulling it taut, the drops slipping down my forearms. If I weren't looking I'd know that they are mine. I move my hands, hold myself up, wash my face, run fingers through my hair. But those large, wide palms, the white fingers, the puffy, meaty wrists, the dimples and scars, the nails that look like mine but are sunken into the flesh – none of that is mine. The fingers are so puffy that I can't quite bring them together. Is it possible I don't know my own hands?

The mirror. I didn't have time to see myself. I still haven't done that. Should I now? Do I dare?

No. I'm afraid. The terror of not recognising myself.

The fear that my eyes won't be the same, that another being will emerge through my skin, appear in my hand, penetrate everywhere. Perhaps it has already spread through my whole body like in horror movies when someone turns into a rat or a vampire before our eyes: hair sprouts on their face, teeth grow longer, nails become claws. They don't notice, but others do and fear. He is already a rat. He is something else. I don't want to be something else.

A long time ago I was able to negotiate with the disease. I'd tell it: 'I'm not going to think about you now, let me rest for a while.' I'd work, read, go to the movies. It would leave me alone for days, sometimes months. Until, passing through a park, I'd stop by a little flowering bush. Light, pink flowers topped with slender tendrils that blossom in a star. Will I be here to see them next year? The question would wash over me suddenly, like their fragrance.

But now I am constantly faced with it. My skin has already taken on a different look, thinner, translucent, scaly like the outside of an onion, taut at my swollen joints and hanging wrinkled from my limbs. When I scratch my head, I find tiny flakes of skin under my nails.

My toes are swollen, almost round. Why did no one tell me about these changes? Warn me? I recognise it. It's water. It seeped into me while I was sleeping, dripped in through the tube, slowly but surely, unstoppable. I hear it swirling around inside me, louder than blood. My heart strains. I feel pressure building under my skin. In my joints. In my eyesockets. Seeking an exit.

It is deforming me, swelling my fingers, bloating my wrists, distending my stomach, making me sick. My belly becomes taut, a hard growth pressing on the incision.

Still dangerous.

I lean over the washbasin and shove a finger down my throat. The water comes out – cloudy, yellowish, foul. Undigested bits of food float in it.

I am enclosed in an unfamiliar form, in untrustworthy hands, in calloused heels, in unshaven armpits, in the muck on my teeth.

Since when did my appearance mean so much? When I was very small I was bothered by the glances of passers-by. I dressed in black, wore trousers and cut my hair short. I never stole mother's lipstick or eyeliner. I didn't try out face powder in secret in front of the mirror. I knew that I would never be as beautiful as she was, with her untouchable glamour. She offered me her clothes, a yellow organdy blouse, a red plaid skirt. New Year's Eve 1965 she lent me a black tulle dress sprinkled with tiny silver specks. It had a stiff petticoat of slippery silk. I put it on and looked in the mirror. The shoulder straps slipped and exposed my bare, bony, unprotected shoulders. My hands were too long and knobbly, my waist too wide, my legs too short. The dress hung in crooked folds like a rag. First I felt envy – the dress fit mother like a glove, glittering, alive. Then I felt contempt for my clumsy body that would never, ever know how to wear ball gowns. I got a stomach ache and gave up on the dress and the party. Lying in bed I listened to the voices, the music, the all-night singing. I grew up quietly contemptuous, separated from my hips and feet, from nylon stockings and bras, perfumes, silk and red lips. I can clearly see the beginnings of the self-denial I later perfected. As if I knew what was to come. I made a division, drew a line between the visible and the invisible and opted for what the eyes could not see. I betrayed my body. Much later it betrayed me.

The body has its own memory.

The contempt that for years I cultivated as my most intimate defence was useful when the disease suddenly attacked. I wouldn't have been able to bear the changes so well, I would have agonised over the gauntness, the exhaustion, the inflammations, the back pain, the nausea. Except at moments of severest pain, I behaved as if it wasn't happening to me. I didn't want to pay attention to it. I didn't speak of it.

The more the sickness attacked me, the more care I took over my appearance. I started to use cosmetics. Gradually make-up became part of my strategy for fooling the disease. 'Good heavens, you look so great, no one would imagine that you were sick.' Each morning I would carefully apply face cream, powder, eyeliner, eyeshadow, mascara, rouge. I covered the traces of dialysis from the previous day, the puffy cheeks, worn-out skin and red eyes. I covered the bags under my eyes with powder, the paleness of my face with rouge, my bloodless lips with lipstick. I achieved the appearance of a carefree, attractive young woman who moves lightly along the street, as on a stage.

Over the mask of death I drew another, more colourful mask. I chased death from me, fooled it, cast spells, wove magic. I thought it was a game that I was playing. A deception.

The colourful mask, that was me, a face on which I wrote out secret signs. My face – my amulet. And only now, when I have lost it, I know that it was mine and I can hardly bear the thought if it turning into something unknown, me turning into someone unknown, into another woman.

All the sudden changes make me insecure. I didn't realise that I had been eaten into from without. I have a hard time thinking 'Me'. I can't see the whole. Inside there are two living halves multiplying like amoeba. Outside, a deformation that blurs the dividing line between body and space. My gaze moves from the blanket to my hand, from my leg to the floor. There is no hesitation, I see no difference in the degree of recognition. I try to convince myself. I strain to see some familiar detail, a birthmark, a scar on my wrist. Or I close my eyes, then it is easier. Except when I see the picture.

First a white piece of paper floats to the surface of my consciousness, then the features of a face come into focus. Pale. Indistinct. The mind, like developing fluid, defines the unknown figure of a woman on the whiteness. Fixed, static, merely present, it means nothing to me. I cannot connect it to my life, I have no memories related to it. I can clearly see that it is a photograph. The mother of some friend of mine? A photograph from a magazine? An album? I shove it back down into the depths, into the darkness. It dissolves and recedes for a short time.

Each time it emerges it troubles me. I contemplate it like an unpleasant, ugly experience that I ought quickly to forget. For some inexplicable reason I seem to feel guilty. I see the woman's smiling face. It is hard to say how old she is – forty, perhaps fifty. She has a stiff, old-fashioned haircut, the kind they still do in small-town salons. They call it a 'perm'. 'Hi, I'd like a perm,' she'd said, before her picture was taken. The woman isn't particularly good looking. She has light eyes and a full face, she seems healthy. American healthy. By her head, to the right but a little lower, is the head of a child – probably a little girl – who does not resemble her. Americans have family photographs on their desks in brass or leather frames. Maybe I saw this one in a place like that, I thought. I didn't know where it had come from. Until I heard.

'Her kidney came from a woman,' the doctor said to someone. He was leaving the room. He thought I was asleep.

When the doctor left the room, his words simply stayed

behind. I couldn't push them out with him.

I didn't want to hear them. I don't care who it belonged to, I am not curious. I think of it as an organ, not as part of a person. I must not be sentimental. My life is on the line. But her picture, reappearing.

Her smiling face, gone forever.

A lot of time will pass, then, in a subway somewhere, a tall man will stop me. (I will have forgotten all about it, the picture will have long since subsided.) He'll say: 'Excuse me, I couldn't help myself, but . . . you look so much like my late wife.' I'll stare at him, indifferent at first. I'll pretend that I have no idea what he is talking about. Perhaps I'll say I don't know any English. But something will force me to change my mind and I'll say: 'Yes. Yes, I probably do look like her. We are sisters, almost twins – you didn't know that she had a sister? You see this thin scar? It has almost disappeared, but this is where she moved in. We live well together, the two of us. Sometimes she gets a little obstinate. I can't keep her from spreading. Sometimes she chooses a smile, other times a gesture, or a walk – to show that she is here, that I am in her power. I think perhaps she wants to make me feel grateful. It's not my fault that she was killed.'

I won't utter any of that. Startled by his own brashness he'll look away from my face and leap through the subway train's closing doors. I will sit on a bench and tremble. Tremble. Tremble. Tremble. I'll forget where it was I was headed. A lost day. When I finally pull together the strength to go out into the daylight, in a store window across the street I'll see my hair has turned completely grey.

My face, my face, I long for it so much! I won't be able to bear this constant search for someone else's presence on it. My means of defence are reduced. I will have to do something soon, put things in order, orient myself, surround myself with familiar things. I don't know what they might be. Perhaps a piece of clothing tossed over the arm of a chair, a newspaper, leftovers from breakfast, the sound of music, voices from the street. This space is not mine, I can't explore it, I can't encompass it with anything. The door that is always open: I am not afraid of someone dropping in unexpectedly, but that something, that barely exists, might escape. Through the window I see a building of dark bricks and an empty construction site. Nine narrow black windows watch me back. Perhaps it is a mistake in the design: long windows that are narrow in the middle and then wider at the top. Or maybe it's a mistake in me. Maybe that building doesn't exist at all. Perhaps it is a memory of warped windows, seen long ago through the thick bottom of a glass, that appears and slides between me and my view every time I glance over there. I believe that complete square chunks of memory can appear, like disembodied television screens or holograms. They can be seen as they float in the air, unreal but moving, alive. A hologram of a kitchen floor: crumbs, dust, cracks between the tiles, a dog's water dish, a recent wet footprint. A hologram of a table, light refracted on its black surface, on a white porcelain swan. I sit there and stretch out my hand for a book: for a moment my hand would be inside the book. I would be inside. Then I'd step through. On the other side would be this hospital room. The hologram as a separate space, a hole, no, a hollow in time. There is nothing behind it. I can only look. But it is not only that, because when I look at it, when I remember, it's as if I string rows of these hollows all around me, tie them together with threads as fine as silk, until they re-form a cocoon.

I must weave circles around myself and maybe that way I can enclose time. Little ones to begin and then larger. Time passes through me. I feel it making me heavy. But I can't hold onto it. I am not in it. There is no Me.

Each time I try to establish continuity I am confronted by a discouraging absence of signs. Is there any certainty here other than pain?

When the morning sun shines through the window of my room in Zagreb, it casts a magnified shadow of the curtain on the wall. Every detail of the white lace is visible. When I wake up, the curtain is an element of stability. I know where I am. There is no break between yesterday and today. Even my dreams are no break, just continuation. Time flows unchecked through the room. The shadows of the curtains slide from one wall to another until they vanish in the darkness that enters from the street.

Fear that I will never make it back there.

3

This yellow room with closed doors where they've moved me. I am a step closer to myself here. I see everything clearly, as if I've just opened my eyes. Crossing the corridor I found myself in a world where everything suddenly became certain: the yellow of the floor, the solidity of the door, the click as it closed. A sensible order reigns here, a calendar on the wall: Tuesday, 11th February. Five days have passed. I woke up and somehow the time had simply vanished. I'll have to tear off the days, one each morning, so in the future I'll know where I am. The sound of paper ripping along the perforated holes will mark the beginning. A morning sound that treats everything that was, whatever it was, as past.

Only bits and pieces surface. How real are they? The lost time is divided into before and after. The between has been amputated, cut off like an arm or a leg or a chunk of the brain and cannot be replaced. How will I overcome this gap, when everything outside me is still without significance, without context, weightless? I might be anywhere. In a hotel, at a friend's house, in some unknown city. I know this is a hospital. While facing inward I don't mind. This room might just as well be floating in space, isolated, separate, like a little box carried by the wind, a bit of nothing. The purity of perception: separate objects, their distinct outlines. The cupboard, television, armchair, table, telephone. When I put books on the cupboard, when I turn on the television and sit in the chair, when the phone rings, then it will be a room. The objects will connect and I will no longer be indifferent. It is important that I can now close the door, lean on the closed door and say aloud, so that I can hear myself: 'My room. This is your room. It has curtains, azaleas, purple tulips, a waste paper basket, soap, glasses.

'You wanted it so, you decided that you had to put a stop to the disintegration.'

The objects possess the required solidity and firmness. It will be easy to lean on them. When you open your eyes they will be here, immobile, fixed securely to the floor. It seems a luxury to have so much furniture around, to notice it so much, to be awake enough to notice it. I can manage that sort of undertaking. Risky, because the disintegration continues. Only the outside world – the fact that it is within reach – can return me to myself. If I convince myself that it is not an illusion, a hallucination, a figment of my imagination, a space arbitrarily inhabited by my memories, then I'll be forced to leave myself and make contact.

I must communicate. With the room. With things. With people. I must try to say what I feel, without holding back. The system that held me back has been shattered.

*

How can I retell what really happened?

I arrived at the hospital. I was operated on. I was in the intensive care unit. Then in room 202. They moved me to room 205. I hardly ever got out of bed, hardly anyone came to visit or called on the phone. Hardly anything happened. Nurses and doctors came in and out. The doors were constantly open. I couldn't get up, then I did get up. That same day I washed my hands and face and sipped a little water, without looking into the mirror over the washbasin.

They have little importance – the visible events and actions that anyone could see.

A camera set up in the room would register closed eyelids, hands moving, the head turning fitfully, then eyes that open and flutter. The expression on the face that can only mean pain. The hurried movements of the hospital staff (injections, oxygen mask, monitoring heartbeat, ECG).

Cut, frame 2: Static, almost frozen. Open, expressionless eyes. Lasts so long that it seems endless. Eyes finally close, which could mean sleep. The staff working with the patient enter the frame from time to time. Two brief visits by women. Her lively reactions, talk, gestures – but the camera does not record sound. Gets up. A few steps around the room and corridor. The central scene goes on in the bathroom. The patient sips a little water, washes her hands then studies them carefully. She washes her face. At one point she starts to look up towards the mirror, but lowers her gaze instantly. She vomits. Hands clutch the edge of the washbasin and she stands there for a long time, with lowered head.

Cut, frame 3: She is in another room, almost identical to

the first. She is sitting on a bed and occasionally reaches decisively for the phone, lifts the receiver then changes her mind.

And the events that preceded this: an attractive woman wearing pink gloves. Grease drips from her hamburger. They have tea and talk. She gets into a taxi driven by a small Chinese man. She gets out of the taxi on a dark street, walks by the doorman and enters a crowded restaurant. A tall blonde woman approaches and tells her something (the film is still silent). She is almost paralysed. Her face: disbelief, shock. The other woman is very excited. She explains something to a small group of people who are sitting around a table, eating. She leaves (all this happens quite fast and a little jerkily, as in a speeded-up silent movie). She sits in a car and drives through the city. She is met at the apartment by a young couple. She rushes to grab a few odds and ends (a book, papers, a tape recorder), makes a phone call, takes a shower, hesitates over a sandwich then finally eats it. She has a beer. All three travel quite far in a taxi. They say very little.

She is alone at the airport. Just before she gets on the plane she makes a phone call. In the plane she drinks a Coca-Cola. The hospital building. The nurse checks the information in the computer and takes her to her room. She takes a blood sample, measures her blood pressure, does an ECG – doctors keep coming in and chatting briefly. Left alone (it is now obvious she is a patient) she writes something, sobs, then takes a few small objects out of her purse and stares at them.

The operating theatre. Classic scenes. The surgeon's

bloody hands. His movements assured.

That is all. It seems as if that is all.

But how can the rest be told? Will the words evaporate into the air, before reaching their destination? I am afraid of my own anxiety – enunciated, named. It will escape through words and spread. It will become visible, palpable, accessible.

My superstition that words call forth events, that they become a separate reality. So final that I shun them. I will turn around and in front of me I will see some other hard, *uttered* life. I won't recognise it.

Fear cannot be expressed. Sickness cannot be expressed. Loneliness is a fine, rigid axis that passes through the core.

This is how it was: when the disease first appeared I was gentle, even grateful. That didn't last long. I figured out how to submit to it superficially, while thoroughly ignoring it at the same time. Have no time to consider it. Distance all emotions – especially hatred – and surround it with coldness. Isolate it like a foreign body, the way certain medicines isolate the cancer cell so that it can't spread any further, before they totally destroy it. To isolate it means to enclose it hermetically in a special inner compartment, not to mention it, certainly not to name it. If necessary, then to use some indefinite phrase containing a negation ('I'm not well') rather than the affirmation ('I am sick'). The meaning seems the same, but it isn't.

The disease had its own tactics. It didn't spread, it didn't get worse, it stayed still. It permitted a balance and controlled the balance. Unnoticed, the isolation that was squeezing the disease began to reflect off it like light from a mirror. It spread and I was the one, not the disease, who was more and more alone, more and more cold. Finally a lump of living matter in a void: I became the disease. Me – disease – me: there ceased to be a distinction.

Now, in this hospital room, I want someone to listen to me, perhaps just to listen, at first. It is easiest to express anxiety over the phone, propped up with pillows, the smooth white receiver against my ear. But could I describe unequivocally what is called my 'reality'? I'd hear my voice leaving me, entering the receiver and drifting further and further away. At the other end it reaches an ear: does it understand? Not understand? Will what emerges really turn into sound? Into words? Even if it does happen, only an analogy is possible, the reality of the words that describes the reality of a person. Noise, voice modulation, accent, sounds, tones, whisper, sob, stuttering, a pause – out of all that you need to decipher meaning. It is quite evident that there would be confusion. Talking into an empty receiver would at first seem a relief: you can't see your interlocutor's face so you aren't afraid. But then you hesitate, you stammer – as when addressing someone who looks past you, staring at a wall, at the floor or into space. No, not the phone.

There again, the person at the other end would hear only the voice. They wouldn't be distracted by the paleness of the skin, the eyes flitting nervously around the room, the hand gestures used for emphasis, the smell of an unwashed body that just lies and sweats, powerless, unhappy. Would they understand me better then? And would I understand their answer – that single stream of messages? When I speak

I must see the person before me, the movements of their pupils, the way they lean towards me, lighting a cigarette, and the way, thoughtful or absent, they absorb themselves in listening.

Jelena dropped in after work. She came in suddenly, tossed her coat on the chair and sat at the foot of the bed. Tired. She still had to pick her son up from school, do some shopping, make dinner (watching the news at the same time on a small television in the kitchen), practise reading with her son, put him to bed, walk nervously around the house and pick up the scattered things, rest her hand on her husband's shoulder, prepare her notes, think a moment before dropping off to sleep that her life consists of a series of unlinked pieces (time, events, people, feelings) and after that, fall into a restless sleep. Then dream that she is in Yugoslavia, in her mother's kitchen. She is making a lemon cake. It is morning, the two of them are drinking coffee. Her mother is whipping up the foamy, pale-yellow cream in a glass mixing bowl and telling her about her father who won't leave his room for days on end. Jelena starts awake with longing. In the darkness of her American bedroom she listens to her husband breathing beside her. She gets up. As her cold feet touch the floor, fleetingly, for a second, she asks herself: Why? Then she pulls the covers up over her child; it is cold outside. She runs her fingers gently through his hair and goes back to bed.

She sleeps a dreamless sleep.

I tell her my dream, about my blood draining out and my mother laughing. My voice was low and, although I hadn't

meant it to be, it sounded as if I were talking about something forbidden.

When I described my mother's laughter, just as I was
saying 'she laughed out loud', I felt with horror that I had
shamed my mother in someone else's eyes.

At the same time I thought that I never should have told
my dream, that I'd be punished. I was sure to be punished!
I'll still be alone, even when everything has been told – or
maybe because of it. I'll still be alone.

At first Jelena sat there quietly, her legs crossed, her
hands resting in her lap, relaxed, as if this were her only
chance to really relax all day. She watched me silently, then
her attention was caught and she leaned forward a little as
if she couldn't quite see me well enough or was seeing me
for the first time. She saw a pale woman sitting on a hospital bed and talking very quietly, not entirely sure that she
wanted someone else to hear. For a moment it seemed to
her that this was no longer the same woman. Something in
her eyes, she thought, the way that she looks past me as she
talks, the tremble in the voice, the long pauses. She never
used to talk about herself – only about her daughter. Last
year, when we went out to buy Christmas presents together, she kept asking me: 'Do you think Natasha would
like this, or this?' Now she doesn't even mention Natasha.
Sometimes I seem to be watching her through my fingers,
that she only permits that kind of perspective. Now the
fingers are spreading apart. This woman is talking about
fear. I'd rather not listen. It threatens me. What has happened? What has broken her so? The operation went
smoothly, everything is fine – but she is not happy. Why is

she talking about her mother? Why is she telling me all this? Is she afraid that we've all abandoned her? Yes. We have. We haven't.

Jelena lifts her hands from her lap and covers her face. She starts to cry. The objects in the room become indistinct once more. 'Ah!' she cries out, with such an effort that the word seems to sting her. She says nothing more, almost nothing more, just 'Ah!' Those two letters. Her hands drop into her lap, fall from her face. She rises to look for a handkerchief. She has to go over to the bureau where she left her bag. For quite a long time she rummages for a handkerchief with her back turned. Wearing a grey woollen sweater that she'd knitted herself, a nondescript skirt, with wool socks and high, flat-soled shoes of light rubber from which a little water drips.

The silence weighs on us. I hear her blow her nose, then the things in her purse rattling: keys, mirror, coins, notes, paper, pencil, comb.

The puddle of water on the floor.

Her back.

It's getting cold and I begin to shiver. I still had time, before she turned towards me, to smooth things over. I could say: 'It was just a dream.' But I couldn't get past the 'just', so I kept silent.

'I brought you some soup,' Jelena says.

She stands with her back turned, her voice hoarse from crying. She turns, smiling. Her eyes betray a trace of pity, but I can bear that now. Jelena takes a red pot from her bag and puts it on the table. Suddenly I feel relief, as if something irreversible had happened. The puddle on the floor

85

was precisely what I needed, so concrete that I noticed that the sky had grown darker in the meantime, that someone had turned all the lights on in the house opposite and the entire scene had come to life. What an astonishing discovery! Outside of me, independent of me, something had happened: it had rained. Jelena had come in and left a wet mark on the hospital room floor – proof of her presence (in the rain, in the room, in the world). If I could sneak out at night, away from sheets that no longer smell of me, put on tall, sensible shoes, lace them up with firm tugs, go out through the doorway and stand. That's all – check whether I can feel the pavement, if I can breathe the air. Does frozen breath come out of my mouth, do my hands get cold? When my fingers got cold I'd blow on them, put my hands in my pockets and go back inside. Carefree because I'd noticed how drops of rain were dripping off my shoes too, running onto the elevator floor, making a brand new puddle.

I exposed myself. The world exists. Somehow, through others, I will get there.

When Jelena left I called Natasha. Now, only now, was I sure I wanted to hear her, that I'd be able to take it.

It was months since I'd left her one early morning in December. I told her I'd be flying early the evening before, that I'd wake her up just to say goodbye. She sat on the couch and watched me as I packed my things in the yellow leather suitcase: one pair of pants, one skirt, two sweaters, a nightgown, stockings, underpants, undershirts. As if the trip was going to be very brief. My gaze kept skipping by her. I was afraid that any minute she might start to cry or that my rhythmic movements might stop her voice as it uttered some ordinary word, cloaking anxiety. 'Have you packed everything? Do you need any help?'

Lost and untalkative she watched me, drinking me in. 'Don't leave me, don't leave me!' But she didn't say it.

In the morning I went into her room. She slept on a low wooden bed, facing the wall. Feeble light filtered in through the skylight. I saw black hair spread over the pillow. The pine floorboards creaked. She turned her head. Under the covers she seemed much smaller, like when I used to get her up for school. She used to say: 'Just five minutes more,' and then would go back to sleep. I found the everyday wrench from sleep hard to bear. I'd rather have left her sleeping, snug, safe. I buried my face in her hair, by her face. The smell. I don't want to forget the fragrance of her soft skin, not fully womanly yet.

Whenever I come back from trips, I always worry that the inevitable metamorphosis may have taken place in my absence. Lightly kissing her cheek I sniff the air, the skin on her neck, with sensitive nostrils like a watch dog. I am guarding her from something inside her, waiting to surface, perhaps right now as I leave.

Tell me to stay and I'll stay. How can I leave you? How could I ever take the smallest trip, around the corner, to the next street, into town? You have an awful power over me, like fire, like a knife. I imagine how I'll see you when I return and how only then, together, we'll be safe. But, if I don't leave now, every new day will bring me closer to death. You sense this, and so you don't say anything.

'Stay in bed,' I told her. 'It's cold outside.'

I wanted her to sleep. Long, long sleep. Deep sleep in which nothing could hurt her.

That would be safest.

'I don't like seeing you off at the airport, mama.'

A child's face, still unworn. My face long gone.

As if I wanted to check on something or maybe reassure myself, I called from the airport. She was already up and surprised to hear from me so soon. She too had begun to practise oblivion.

They showed a movie on the plane about a newspaper-man from the *Village Voice* who was in love with an aerobics instructor. I forced myself to watch it carefully. I thought about how Jamie Lee Curtis has a marvellous body and then took a sleeping pill and stretched out over two seats. Just before I drifted off, I saw the sea shore and a boat. The tiny boat.

I woke up over New York at two in the afternoon. My watch told me it was eight in the evening. Natasha was eating dinner, I was having lunch.

Apart already.

I called her regularly, as if a routine could make up for absence. Beyond a certain point, all that is left is the slender thread of telephone conversations, listening for a tremble in the voice, a silence that betrays an intention completely different from the words being said. 'Everything is fine,' we repeated, carefully avoiding a truth that neither of us dared utter: that she had nothing to fall back on, that she had to turn the heating on herself and buy her own bread. She doesn't know whether it will always be that way or not.

From week to week she learned to lie and kept getting better at it. She didn't want to tell me how before going to school each morning she'd crouch over the toilet and strain to vomit, but she couldn't.

For months she will grow up alone, smoking forty cigarettes a day, living on sandwiches or nothing at all, bleeding almost constantly. A rash of tiny watery blisters will break out again on her hands. They will itch and turn into scabs before her skin peels and flakes away, leaving red patches of flesh covered with a thin film of skin. She will wrap finger after finger in bandages so she won't bite them. Her hands will be bound with bandages as she moves about town, as if she has been wounded in some invisible war.

'Mama.'

I hear her voice over the telephone, thinner and more gentle than I remember. I feel my whole body straining to be with her.

She says the word without query, without doubt. She was waiting for me to call.

'Mama.'

Her voice, that word, the expectation: I haven't the strength here to be a mother, just a child. A curled up, drowsy child who has trouble remembering her past. What Natasha wants to hear from me, I want to hear from my own mother. The three of us are like a triple mirror. I see them both reflected in me, bound together by our multiple reflections. Do we exist otherwise? I can't think about them. I can't think about her, how she stands there in the middle of the night, barefoot on the tiles in her undershirt. Waiting for the phone to ring. I ought to tell her that I'm doing well.

'I'm fine.'

It sounds sad.

I'm tired. I'm so tired.

It seems that I hear her breath near me, but it is the noise of the ocean between us.

'Don't hang up yet.'

I don't hang up, not yet. I am afraid of that silence, so powerful. Maybe she's crying, covering the receiver with her hand so I won't worry. We speak tersely, shyly. I tell her to look both ways when she crosses the street. She laughs, cheerfully, as if that is exactly what she was waiting for.

I carry a picture of her like a St Christopher. In it she is three years old, with blonde curly hair and a solemn face. That was spring of 1971. In her hand she clutches a little woollen dog. I had her picture taken at a shop with a sign outside saying Photographic Studio.

I wanted to capture her, freeze her, keep her forever, so tiny and serious, in a blue dress with yellow knitted knee socks. Hold her hand when she crosses the road, forever. My time and hers stopped at the Photographic Studio, under lights that illuminate the details of her frightened little face, her eyes that look for me beyond the pool of light and can't find me. She stood like that for a moment, brightly lit. It looked as if the light was spreading from her, through her skin, she was so pale. At that perfect moment I clearly saw every strand of her pale hair, her grey, slightly-slanted, yellow-flecked eyes, an agitated blue vein pulsing in her left cheek, her compressed lips, a little crooked as if she wants to cry but controls herself because of me, round shoulders in a yellow cotton shirt. Child-like arms, pudgy fingers and dimples where her joints should be. She held the one-eared grey toy dog – her only stronghold.

I was standing outside the pool of cold light, in the dark, invisible to her. The sharp border between us, a separateness at the edge of light. Our two skins were once one.

At that moment I knew what it meant to be a mother: watching a child grow, knowing what it means.

Suddenly I am overwhelmed by anxiety. I hate her for that. I hate her because I am completely hers, because I know that I can belong so completely only to her, now and forever.

Outside it was sunny. That isolated circle of light and time ceased to exist except in my memory. I remembered the swirling particles of dust in a beam of light, the grey linoleum floor, the squeaking of the swivel chair on which she sat, swinging her feet high above the chrome crossbars. And the ceiling fan, blinds for the spotlights, the black curtain heavy with the smell of acid – a frontier that only sometimes we can cross, if allowed. I carried her all the way home in my arms along a quiet street, through a row of birches that had just sprouted pale green leaves. No one had ever seemed more fragile. I wanted her back in my womb, rocking her in the soft darkness where only blunted echoes of the outside world could penetrate.

I seem to feel better now. It is morning. The 'recovery' is going according to schedule. From time to time I feel capable of recognising its different elements, its rhythm or pro-

gress. At other times recovery just seems an empty statement, because I feel nothing of the sort. Doctors visit me
several times a day. In the early morning, while I'm still
quite groggy from the sleeping pills, the door will open,
light will glare and the on-duty doctor asks if everything is
all right before moving quickly on. Later several of them
come. Dr Weiss: I make an effort with him; I hope I sound
cheerful, optimistic. He seems pleased.

That is how I get reinforcement. Maybe. Yes, reinforcement. For those few minutes I am concentrated, suspi-
ciously aware of his every movement: the raised eyebrow,
the inquisitive gaze over the glasses, a finger to the lips,
hurry or hesitation. With practised eyes I catch those signs
in order to find something out about myself. Am I well? Are
my physical functions working properly? And as soon as he
leaves I forget what we talked about. What did I say? What
did they say? I am still in their hands, like a being that's not
yet human, from which they are constantly taking blood
tests, changing the intravenous needle, changing the bed-
ding, changing everything. They bring in a tray with little
plastic dishes containing thin green fluids, crumbs of grated
carrot, macaroni in an unappealing brown sauce or long
pieces of fried fish. The prettiest is the raspberry jelly, like a
shiny dark red cube of glass or a huge ruby. It can't be edi-
ble. Everything tastes the same anyway, even the orange
juice in the clear plastic cup, even the cup itself. You
should drink more, the nurse says, and takes away the tray,
food untouched. I am still an object in my own recovery,
not so much uninterested as surprised that all this is going
on without my involvement, without my will. I can't follow

the speed with which the colour of my skin is changing, the number of red blood cells growing, the incision healing, pain diminishing. I am becoming aware of a feeling of tightness in that place.

The nurse brings in a computer sheet and reads out my results. They are excellent. Everyone is delighted, as if my health was their personal concern. Dr Weiss asks: 'How do you feel?'

I don't know how I feel.

I feel as if I'm multiplied. As if you have removed my brain. I think I feel like raspberry jelly, a transparent, dark red mass shuddering on the bed. Then it stretches, spreading across the floor, climbing the walls and ceiling until it covers everything in a fine film. Wrapped around objects, it melts them like acid. It absorbs their substances to feed its empty, transparent insides.

I am not here. I'm like the old woman sitting on the tram. It rushes along the streets. Out the window pictures of houses, people, sky and trees dash by. She sees it all, but only sees. She is not there: the random pictures do not penetrate to a point where they would acquire meaning, fit into a scheme, become important. They don't tell her anything. They slip between the covers of a finished photograph album, there to reside. I feel like those watery, pale eyes of hers, the dissipated pupils, eyes that recognise outlines here and there but not their meaning. Reality is still only a charming game where light and colour mingle without understanding. Her being is crumbled into dust, unrecognisable objects left in drawers. The body is a form in which she only partly resides: that meaningless body, already melting into its surroundings, is equally foreign and insensitive; there is no distinction. She could abandon it at any time, leave it behind to sit there a while longer, until the tram suddenly brakes and it flops forward, leans its forehead on the man in the seat in front. After a while the man would turn around and discover with horror that he had just been touched by death. At the next stop he'd hurriedly leave the tram, but the weight would rest a while longer on his shoulders. Like a shroud.

The old woman only seems to be still sitting on the tram. Her body is expiring. The thin, rigid skin still holds back the already advancing disintegration, wrinkled on the finger joints as if they need special protection. She had time to grow ugly, wrinkled, dried up, to gradually petrify. She had time to grow dull, become disgusting, link images without sense, close all passages except her eyes. She had time. I ride beside her, equally undone, with smooth skin and lively eyes. Each thing I see has a special importance: I may be seeing the chestnut tree for the last time, the green window of a shoe repair shop and three pots of flowers outside an attic apartment by the tram stop. My eyes are first greedy then indifferent, blind to the awareness that I haven't time, that I won't have time to get ready. No matter how diligently I practise, I can't match the old lady's dull peace of mind, no longer thinking about time because she is beyond it.

I am overwhelmed by a physical longing to become the old woman riding on the seat in front of me, switching the load to the back of the young man in front of her. He stops on the street for a moment and looks back.

Unsure. Totally unsure.

*

I still have to separate my body from its surroundings, un-
glue it from the things that stick to it firmly when it's
awake, afraid that it will dissipate. But this goes slowly and
it is hard. I keep getting lost. In bed I drift off into a doze
from which I wake up even more tired and I have to get
used to the surroundings all over again. They give me pills,
but the pills make dreams into nightmares. I can't slip into
a deep, sound sleep. On waking I lie with my eyes closed, as
if I'd rather endure the nightmare than be looking constantly around me with effort. It's true I'm walking again,
without support. That certainly means something. When I
walk, I have to do so cautiously so that I don't trip. I can
already get from the door to the window or to the bathroom. And yesterday they took the catheter out of my bladder. I lay on the bed with legs wide apart. First the nurse
let the air out of the balloon that kept it from falling out
when I move and then, with a quick jerk, she removed the
rubber tube. I winced. It didn't hurt though I was ready for
the pain anyway. She showed me the tube, pleased as if this
were some joint venture of ours. 'We've gotten this far,' she
said, 'now you'll find it much easier.' I smiled. I couldn't
figure out what she was talking about. How far had we
gotten?

'You should go to the bathroom, urinate.'

She said it as if she was absolutely certain that at that
moment I had to urinate, as if it was suddenly definite and
self-evident. Didn't she know that patients like me never
urinate more than a few drops that they can hold back or
let go at will? Pressure on the bladder becomes a strange,

forgotten feeling.

My stomach muscles are tense. I feel a little discomfort. It must be from the catheter.

'I don't need to go,' I said.

She took me by the hand, helped me get up and sat me on the toilet like I was some singularly stubborn child and she knew better than I did whether I had to go or not. I was left there, sitting on the toilet in a half-dark bathroom, my nightgown pulled up high. The dull pain in the depths of my stomach didn't relent. I knew that all I had to do was relax my muscles and it would go away. But I couldn't. I didn't. I sat there clutched, holding onto my stomach with both hands. Drops of sweat rolled onto my knees.

I was afraid to urinate.

No, I feared something else: that I'd relax, that I'd try to urinate and then I'd only have a few drops, like before. I was afraid of defeat, vain effort, a futile operation, the return to dialysis.

If I could only put off that moment, defer it as long as possible, until I had the strength to bear the possibility of defeat. Only now had everything come to a head: not in the waiting room, not in the operating theatre. Now. Through the closed door I could hear voices in the corridor, footsteps, the sound of wheels turning, music from a radio, nurses calling to one another. The food trolley went by. Someone washed their hands and repeatedly, impatiently, pushed the lever for soap. From the next cubicle I heard the flushing of water and the creaking of a door.

Then I heard a strikingly new sound, different from all the others. The sound of my own urinating. A sure, long stream. I grabbed the handle on the wall, lifted myself and turned on the light. Standing with legs astride, I leaned forward. The broad stream of dark yellow urine cascaded down the porcelain toilet bowl, colouring the water at the bottom. I stood up straight. The warm liquid ran down my thighs, mixing with the sweat. I still hadn't finished urinating. Water was gushing from me. I put my hand under the stream: it filled my fist, seeped through my fingers and overflowed onto the floor.

It smelled like ammonia. Like dirty laundry. Like intimacy.

Here, above this toilet bowl in a smoothly tiled bathroom, I realised a miracle had happened – and that this miracle was indissoluble, one, mine alone.

I tensed my muscles, the stream stopped flowing. I relaxed them. The stream started flowing again.

I toyed with it.

Completely alive: golden, roundly alive.

4

I splayed my arms in the bathroom with my palms against
the wall. Across from me I saw a woman laughing. She
laughed aloud, her head flung a little back – young, untidy,
no make-up. Her greasy hair hung lank on her shoulders
and around her almost round face. She laughed strangely,
one lip twisted downward at the corner as if she was about
to cry. When she noticed me she slapped her hand abruptly
over her mouth, then let it drop falteringly from her face
with a trace of doubt, or perhaps surprise. She came closer
and stared into my eyes. I felt as if I might speak, that she
might ask: 'Do I know you?' I seem familiar to her, she
looks me over with a long, greedy gaze. She weighs me up
like a piece of meat. Her eyelids are swollen. She has dark
bags under her eyes, eyebrow hairs sprouting far under the
drawn lines. The skin on her face is splotched with dry,
pink spots. She's a mess. This woman has stopped looking
after herself.

Why does she look like this?

Does she have the faintest idea what she looks like?

I ran my fingers through my hair.

In the mirror a hand rose in an arc, with a slow, entranced gesture, suddenly unsure whether she – her hair – were really there. I felt how oily it was beneath my fingers. My face. There, in the mirror, I see my face. She is still smiling, her teeth gleam. That woman must have been in here with me from the start. In the room, in bed, on the toilet, in the bathroom. And now here she is simply standing before me, solemnly watching with a frozen smile. The face is shared by the woman watching me and the woman I watch. Bits and pieces of Me, and me within it as in a makeshift shelter. Her face seeks some sign of recognition in my eyes. So visibly split in two. I see her, trembling uncertainly, refusing to recognise herself. Her eyes drift from the surface. I pull into myself deeper and deeper, as if moving from a larger skin into a smaller one, from a larger box into a smaller one, while the breach between them grows, wide open space. As if I am little – how I yearn to be little. A row of hollow wooden dolls, packed one inside the next. The smallest is the best protected, but it cannot get out until each of the outward figures is pulled apart, destroyed. Each scale, each skin, each layer, each membrane.

I entered the slowly smiling woman, the lids dropped, the parts fit together snugly. Now, with great effort, I can read the trace of metamorphosis on her face, on my face. I study it closely once more.

To face one's final layer of self and be aware that only a few precarious bridges and tentative ties remain between inside and outside.

That doesn't matter any more, I thought, that will never

matter as *much*. Now this body system functions differently. I can relax. It is finished.

But I am still standing barefoot in a puddle of tepid urine, slowly growing cold.

Every once in a while, unexpectedly, this savage feeling of existence comes over me. Like when I'm on the street, in broad daylight, walking through a crowd, and suddenly I see my face in a shop window. Or when in the morning I pour coffee into a cup in the kitchen. Its fragrance wafts around me and I think about how splendid it is that I exist. And the coffee. And the cup.

That feeling undoes me. Because of it I carry a vague burden in my breast for ages, a shadow of doubt, the fear that it will be terribly hard to die afterwards. When the moment of bald existence has passed, I am more aware of my fragility, my longing, stirring and lunging.

I become greedy. I lie awake long into the night. I listen to sounds, listen feverishly. I can't bear to miss the rustling of leaves on the ash tree, the plunk of chestnuts dropping to the ground, the distant croaking of a frog. A late bus stops at the corner, people get off, footsteps. Conversation freezes in the night air. Fragments suspended like icicles hanging from branches before crashing to the sidewalk under the window. I lie still, hardly breathing, wanting to maintain the imagined equilibrium. I feel less and less a part of the pulsation, the general noise, as if I'm absent, but yet so full of longing . . .

Then I practise. I leave myself completely, looking down on my motionless body, and with childlike relief I see that everything is the same, everything. Nothing has changed, my leaving wouldn't change anything. The window is open a crack and sounds continue to come into the room. The house is calm. The clock in the kitchen strikes loudly. The gas meter is buzzing. It will be light soon. But the body slowly stiffens. I think how horrible it is, but at the same time I force myself to consider how easy it would be to leave. It must be easy. And while I think that, I hear my breathing – lightly, very quietly, a soothing sound – and it frightens me, because I will never, never, never relinquish that.

I wake up. By the window opposite the bed stands a small plastic basket of strawberries. Hannah came. 'What would you like me to bring?' she had asked me. Something magical, impossible, forbidden. Outside my world. A step with which I'll underline the change.

'Strawberries. Bring me strawberries, please.'

Hannah spent thirty years in Czechoslovakia, she has only recently come back to the United States. Only she would understand this powerful urge – strawberries in February! In Czechoslovakia, in Yugoslavia, they ripen in May and are only bought for children. Here I first saw midwinter strawberries on a supermarket shelf. Standing in my winter coat, gloves, scarf, shoulders wet from snow.

They look plastic, I thought, offended by the idea that you can buy them here any time. Strawberries in November, strawberries in August. Does anyone ever really crave them here?

Now I want them. Is it hunger? No, not yet, that too is a matter of decision. For several days they have been standing on the windowsill, one of the objects surrounding me. I have learnt not to see them as food, along with chocolate, or bananas, or tomatoes. I used to walk through the fruit and vegetable section at the supermarket as through a museum, looking at the colours of a still life: the green of the spinach, dark purple aubergine hues. Before me lay tender cabbages, grapes, wrinkled dates and peppers with perfectly taut skins, lifeless, pithed. Every day as I passed I practised self-denial, like a painter who uses only shades of white. Not through dislike of the rest of the colours, but because she is forced to, because she defends himself that way. Colours devastate her system.

Hannah took the basket of strawberries out of a brown paper bag and placed it on the table between us. She handled it gingerly, like something valuable that sudden movements might damage. We looked at the strawberries and neither of us moved.

For Hannah it is as if she is still in Prague and going to the marketplace on a chilly, foggy April morning. She strolls thoughtfully from counter to counter, seeing the little piles of potatoes, cabbages, onions and winter lettuce. She wears white woollen socks that she has knitted herself. She notices that new potatoes have come in – tiny, clean, almost skinless. And the slender green pods of the first peas. But she doesn't go too close. She buys a few heads of lettuce and some winter potatoes. As she weighs each one in her hand she sees they are already wrinkled and sprouting, some of them frostbitten. She thinks how she'll add eggs and make a moussaka with lots of spice to cover their sweetness, the flavour of winter. On her way out of the marketplace she buys two bundles of spring onions with tapering greens. Her conscience bothers her: she won't tell them at home about the new potatoes and the peas, she'll put them off a little while longer. But the onions – she'll chop them up into a bowl of hard winter lettuce.

In Zagreb, Natasha would be eating lettuce when suddenly she tastes a new taste in her mouth.

Just when she thinks she has bought all she needs Hannah notices a queue. There are strawberries on a stall at the other end of the marketplace. Maybe a dozen shallow wooden crates. He'll sell them all by nine o'clock and anyone coming later to market won't even know the strawberries were ever there. Unless they notice the scent: she smelt them first, so brazenly fresh. Hannah hadn't seen them yet this year. She came closer to the counter: they were small and stuck with clumps of soil. It rained recently. The young woman whose turn it was in line asked for half a pound and the assistant scooped them up clumsily, cutting several in half, exposing them – pale pink hearts. The aroma thickens. They are still too expensive, Hannah thought. She hesitated. Well, what about a few? Not for herself, for Andrei. When he comes home from school she will give them to him (putting away half for tomorrow) in a glass bowl, with sprinkled sugar. She'll push them across the table with a calculatedly nonchalant gesture as if she does it every day. As if it is nothing. As if they were in America.

Then no, not today.

Tomorrow, if she can. You have to be strong for that performance.

I sit opposite her, opposite Prague, opposite the market

103

and the strawberries. I always buy the first strawberries for Natasha, because she has no father and I don't know how to tell her, now that she's seventeen, that I love her.

'I can't eat them,' I say.

Hannah puts them back on the windowsill without a word.

Perhaps it would be best to hurry and drink Jelena's beef soup right away, before the transparent layer of yellow fat congeals. Utter familiarity, so familiar that I can't get lost. Something to melt the cloying insecurity on my palate. Grasp the spoon and taste: the soup must be hot. I crumble the dark bread Jelena left in a plastic bag by the soup pot. In Zagreb, I muse, the bread would be wrapped in a linen napkin. In Boston Jelena bakes bread on Saturdays, her kitchen hot and fragrant. Aroma seeps out the windows, through the doors, descends the stairwell to the front hall where it stays closed up all afternoon. After taking the long, thin, dark loaves sprinkled with sesame seeds out of the oven, she lines them up on the table to cool and covers them with a white dishcloth. I can see her hand take the large black-handled knife to cut a slice. She rummages in the drawer for a bag to put it in. At class she tells students about the functions of the left and right halves of the brain, about the holograms of memory. The soup and bread stand on the floor, in her bag.

I eat the concept of soup, its security. The yellow, greasy rim remains round the edge of the plate. I scoop up soaked chunks of bread with a big spoon and gulp them greedily down, listening to how the soup sloshes over my tongue,

down my throat and into my stomach. There it is channelled. Already I feel it in my bloodstream, no longer just
salty water dripping down the tube, through the needle,
into my hand, into my blood. Heat permeates me.

As long as I eat this way, somehow I'm safe.

Years ago in a different hospital I watch my mother pour
soup from a thermos into a plastic hospital plate scratched
by aluminium spoons. The floor is red cement, several
drops have splashed on it. Big, black cockroaches emerge
from a crack in the wall at night to eat. I hear them scurry-
ing around, their little legs scraping the wall, the door, the
legs of the bed. They scamper across the slippers to the bin,
they climb up on the table. Some of them fall, plop!

During the day the balcony door is left open, the heat
comes in. The hospital is up on a hill and you can see the
sea and grey boats inching along the horizon. Fine, hand-
cut noodles float in the soup for that is all I can eat. She
brings the soup every day: there are no refrigerators here.
Even if there were, the nurses wouldn't be allowed to heat
the food, it is forbidden. Visits are allowed at 3 pm. She has
to climb up the street that twists uphill, bringing the thermos bottle, a towel, pyjamas, a newspaper, a roll and two
ironed handkerchiefs folded in triangles. The street is
empty, there is no shade. She climbs slowly but not so
slowly that the soup will get cold. As I eat my teeth are
numb from the aluminium spoon. The soup leaves a ring
round the dirty white rim.

Food, overwhelming me. Maybe this is the only way left
for me to apprehend reality, the body.

On the sill, a can of beer, a lemon, a yoghurt – what

opulence! I am suddenly surrounded by luxury. Curtains, a bouquet of full-blown yellow roses, a bottle of white wine. The nurse heated Jelena's soup in the kitchen in a microwave oven. There is a refrigerator in there with milk, orange juice, apple juice, prune juice. 'You don't have prune juice in Yugoslavia?' she asks, unsure just where and what Yugoslavia is. Around me there are plastic cups, paper cups, a menu, a styrofoam disposable plate, napkins, coffee, tea, ice from an icemaker, handkerchiefs soaked in alcohol for disinfection, gauze, plasters, sterile gloves, masks, paper tissues.

Suddenly I seem to have everything I could want, more than I need. The soup's greasy rim expands to encompass the entire room. It becomes stuffy as if a whole crowd of people is breathing its air.

The crowd follows my every movement.

They watch my pleasure as I eat, as I bring the spoon to my mouth, as I move my jaw and swallow. I know they are here. I pretend not to notice them. If I look up, they will talk. I'll hear their voices, distant or long since silent. They have been lying in wait for me. They jostle to get closer. Closer still. They watch. If I were to stretch out my hand, I could touch their cold, transparent bodies. Is there anything that can shield me from them? Is there anywhere I can hide? They are strong, they break down all walls. Faces emerge from the dark and strain towards me. They watch hungrily. I feel the saliva collecting in their mouths. I eat even faster.

They are drooling, damp rises from my feet, I feel cold, suddenly, alone. Around me stand the white, empty beds on which they used to lie.

– Zdenka, who did her own dialysis in her apartment, knitting or peeling apricots to make jam. 'Never waste a moment,' she said, and even talked about adopting a child. The inflammation of the brain lasted just a few days. She thought it was only a bad headache. It was already too late by the time she got to hospital.

– Jasna, whose husband left her when he found out she was sick. She moved in to her mother's with her daughter. She went to dialysis for barely six months. Each time she would throw up. I looked away. One Sunday she went to Belgrade. On Monday she was late for the morning train – intentionally, perhaps? On a bus at noon she was already feeling unwell. The bus drove across the plains, the fields crept slowly by. By the time she got to Zagreb she was in a coma. So pale.

– Daniella, who was twelve, with thin arms and bulging blue veins. First she limped, then they put her in a cast. At night she screamed with pain. 'Her bones are coming apart,' the doctor told her mother who travelled over seventy miles every day to see her. Later Daniella stopped recognising her. They gave her morphine. Her heart, it seemed, couldn't take it.

– Ante was so light that his petite wife could pick him up out of his wheelchair and put him on the hospital bed. She was a cleaning woman. Mornings she worked and in the afternoons took him to the park to enjoy the fresh air among the children. But he kept on shrinking. She cried ahead of time.

– Mr Zečević, who said of himself that he was old,

although he was only sixty. He was old because he was alone. His wife jumped out of a window when she heard that he was sick too. She already had cancer. He didn't last long: an operation, a stroke. They brought him down to dialysis unconscious. When he revived I wanted to tell him something nice. I didn't know what to say. I asked, 'How are you?' He stared at me, distraught. He kept crying his last few days. He didn't want to die in a hospital.

– Branka. Her husband left her, too. She was left with her son and mother, living off her mother's pension. She grew crazier as time passed. She heard voices, shouted: 'I know you want to kill me!' She wrenched the needle from her arm. Blood spurted. She was operated on. Three months later the kidney ceased functioning. Her mother died. She was left alone and couldn't bear it. Now she is in an asylum. Her son is fourteen and lives alone. The neighbours say that he still goes to school.

– Vanja was eighteen when she first came to the hospital. They thought that it wouldn't last too long. She sat on a chair as her mother painstakingly braided her long hair. As if, when braided, it could never be undone.

They press up against me and, if I let them approach, there will be no air left at all.

Let me be. I don't know you any more. I must forget you. It is not my fault, it is not my fault.

But it is my fault because I lied, I pretended to understand you, that we were in the same boat. I comforted you. I urged you to hope for something, telling you that everything would be fine. Now I am sitting here, chewing bread – the sole survivor – loudly sipping delicious soup. I crumble Jelena's bread. I have strawberries on the windowsill, my eyes are shiny from the beer. What a harsh deception. I knew the system of the split, of turning off. I was always in a good mood – didn't you find that suspicious? Didn't you sense that there was another reality from which you were totally, perfectly excluded? Didn't you know that you were only shades from a nether world on which I had carefully closed the door? I asked you how you were feeling and didn't listen to the answer. I didn't want to care. What a cruel selfishness – and how I now love that cruel selfishness that will pale your faces.

I'll forget you, I'll forget.

Leave me alone.

But father remains. I can't chase him away.

He sits alone on the chair by the window, wearing pyjamas with grey and blue stripes, pulling his dry, bony skull between his shoulders. Hunched over, he smokes by the window though he's sensitive to cold. Last year, they removed his new kidney after only a month. It had turned into infected mush. He thought he was dying and begged them to put him out of his misery. Yet he is alive. He can sit and smoke a cigarette.

Does he envy me?

Does he remember that he is my father, the father of my disease?

I have so many photographs hanging on the walls, framed, glazed. I convince myself that he exists. I keep what little I have of his so it won't vanish: a trace of similarity, a hand holding mine. There is not a single picture of just the two of us: only father alone, father and mother, father and brother, or all four of us. He stands in his naval uniform by a black car holding my brother. My brother is a year old. Mama and I are inside. It is hot, but the windows are up. Separated by the window, we remain in the background, a part of the landscape. As if we inhabit only that internal, glassed-in world. Our features can be discerned from outside – blurred, incomplete faces on which lines are hardly visible. The sun is shining and, compared to us, father and brother are in sharp focus against the blue background. Although she knows that her smile can hardly be seen, mother smiles. I still haven't learned that I should smile, too. I don't want to be behind the glass, I want to hug my father around the neck and fall asleep there.

A year earlier. The kitchen floorboards were scrubbed and damp. The white dust of summer had settled on my child's shoes. Father stood by the window. When I came in, he smiled and pressed me to him as if he hadn't seen me for a long, long time. He was wearing a white, sleeveless undershirt. I leaned my head on his bare shoulder. It smelled of carbolic Jelen soap.

'You have a little brother now,' he said.

Later, much later, I needed proof to believe that this unknown man was my father. I couldn't believe mother. Or myself. I hung his pictures up on the wall, his life. I thought how dry the word 'father' sounds, how it means so little.

Or it means: cold, fear.

He's looking at me now. Squinting from the light, silent. 'Say something. Tell me what it was like when you . . .'

Silence.

And now? The silence between us is too wide. I will never bridge it. I hear dust settling from the ceiling. The white dust is shaken from my child's shoes. Tiny particles float like fine rain, filling the room, obscuring him. I wave but it is too late. He can no longer see or recognise me. He doesn't see that I've stood up and started towards him: 'Don't leave, please don't, forgive me, I never pushed you away, stay, stay!' But he moves off, slipping with the chair through the mist in the depths of the room, this or some other, perhaps a third. I am frightened that he'll bump into something and that it will be the end, but he slows down and passes through the wall. At the last moment he raises his right hand in parting as if he has just remembered something.

I shout helplessly after him.

But he's gone.

He sits on his apartment balcony staring at the sea. Night, the waves glisten. He wanted to travel, he didn't travel, now he doesn't care. He gets up, goes into the kitchen. A plate is on the table, dinner. Pasta. The table is covered with a white tablecloth. He sits before a white plate with white pasta, a knife in his right hand. The knife is heavy. It weighs him down with its senseless heaviness, a blade with nothing to cut.

How wrong that is, he thinks, to cut pasta with a knife.

How wrong it all is.

His gaze moves across the smooth, black and white concrete floor, the white cupboards hanging on the wall, the white refrigerator. There is not a single glass in the sink. There are no curtains on the windows. The kitchen is perfectly clean, unrecognisable, cleansed of him, as if he is already gone. Soon the invisible hand will wash the knife he is holding, and the plate and the glass. It will wipe away his footsteps from the floor, the trace of his fingers on the door. No sooner does he touch them than the traces vanish. Each thing he touches immediately melts like snow. He no longer knows what to do with himself. He wanders around the house like a ghost. He eats less and less, becoming progressively invisible. Occasional visitors trip over him and are surprised. Father thinks: Now, when I should say something, I don't know. And what should I tell her?

Should I tell her how I yearn to drink my fill of goat's milk and then ride a bicycle the three miles into town, along the twisting slopes, with my trouser legs held by a clothespin?

I sense that he knows something I don't.

I sense he knows the answer to my questions, but I can't get through to him.

Later, I sit in my room, carefully cutting strawberries into thin, transparent slices, thinking about my guilt and how I've triumphed. And then how I've betrayed even him, as well as the others. The few things that held us together have disappeared: disease, submission, the slender thread of blood. His absence strengthens, he is freezing. A desert in me spreads. Melting on my tongue, the strawberries fill me with the red taste, I am present in the taste.

Presence, undermined by a sense that I have stolen something from somebody.

This sense of guilt disturbs me.

Float. Forget what has happened inside. Do simple

things. Do nothing at all. Not feel. Grow completely still, then listen closely.

I'll give up. I can't bear this tension, those memories. The horror is no longer on the skin, on the face I don't recognise. It's invisible now, enclosed in cellular nuclei, in blood, in veins, coursing through my abdomen, curled in a cold ball in my gut.

There is an alien horror in my stomach that I must tame. I feel it rear wildly, my gut pushing it to the surface in convulsive waves, towards the taut skin, stretched but painless. The stitches will simply open and with one shudder the stomach muscles will reject that chunk of foreign tissue.

I am feverish. The chill starts in my right flank and radiates out. This foreign piece of flesh that I am fighting against. Fighting for. Foreign. Stolen. Abducted. Whose? If I only knew whose, maybe it would be easier. No, it wouldn't be easier. I don't want to know anything. Why must I fight? My will, my control – it is too late for that. Waves of fever wash over me in the darkness, in a nightmare, in a dream. As I sink, I ask whether it all makes sense but the question is meaningless and it sinks into the darkness with me. My body now struggles alone, utterly alone. I rest my hand on my stomach, then the pillow. I want to plug the hole that threatens to gape, but I'm already asleep. Someone takes me by the hand and I lightly get down from the bed as if weightless or as if weight no longer matters. It is someone old, I can't see his face, just the grey hair and proffered hand, the fingers he touches me with. I cross the room with sure, rapid steps, then my steps turn into leaps and pirouettes and I rush on and on, into the black space where everything is possible. I seem to hear his voice, but it is blurred. I know he stands by my bed and protects me. I know that the fever will soon subside, maybe before morning.

Morning will enter and find a body that is resting from its struggle in an empty room. The pillow will still be pressed against the stomach. At the same time, entering the room next door, pale grey light will bathe the man who is lying motionless, as if dead. But he will sigh with relief and it will sound like fog, an aggressive explosion, from which the body in the next room will start in its sleep. That is the price, the motionless man may think, the price for holding my eyes open, to see the pale light that is filtering into the room, to move my hand a little and press the button to call the nurse. The nurse will come in and say 'Good morning'. She'll prop him up with pillows and then with a mask on her face and her hands in thin rubber gloves she will clean the mucus build-up at the opening in his neck through which a wide, transparent tube enters. Her movements will be gentle, or at least it will seem so to him. The tube is like a fluted paper accordion, a pale green Chinese lantern. Its thin membranes stretch, each exhalation straining them. When she first came in to him, the nurse wondered how long he could survive like this, how he could bear it, unable to speak or walk. He saw the question in her eyes. He had learned to spot it on the face of whoever was first to stop in or glance through the open door. Meanwhile she stopped asking. She knew that he wasn't bearing it; that was his life. He watches the morning light as it encroaches on the room and thinks how good it is. To see. To hear. The sound of his own breathing through the tube that they change once a week fills him with a sense of security, much like the rhythmic beating of the heart. I breathe, he thinks – he no longer tries to speak, gurgling is all that would be heard – I am here. Then he watches television: a woman in a bathing suit brings a tall glass of yellow beverage to her mouth and smiles at him. He smiles back. Hawaii, palm trees, all those healthy, fresh people. The ease with which they move about on the glittering beaches. They eat, kiss, say unimportant sentences. He likes being in the company of the tiny people on TV, their pointless movements, their simple pain.

An old Polish woman sits by him in the room, pale, her skin the pale green of a climbing vine. She sits quietly with a gaping, toothless jaw. Only her bony hand moves. The skin hangs from her in transparent folds. Completely separate, like levers, her hands shovel food into her funnel-like mouth. Noiselessly, she swallows. Her eyes are motionless. The last thing she can remember is the bombing of Warsaw. Houses disappear as she stands in the middle of the street and waits until it is her turn to melt – this is the end. The end. But the end is far off, the hand-lever feeds automatically. Sometimes she sits in the corridor in a wheelchair and sucks up air with an equally gaping mouth – because there is no other answer, grab at the air no matter how, with gaping jaws, through plastic tubes, it makes no difference. But to see, take part, be able to be here, in a room with a window, in a brightly-lit corridor, where people walk by.

Day has not yet dawned.

I listen to voices. Between the velvet dark that pulls me to it and the effort of the body to wake up, I hear them talking about a crisis. A light touch of a hand to my forehead. She has a fever. And then a voice from above, from heights at which it is already morning and everything is clear, explicable.

'Do you want this kidney or don't you?'

I want it, but I'm afraid. Will it always be so foreign?

When I'm walking along will I press the place with my hand? Will I think of it at every step? Will I be afraid of crowds, being jogged, a fall? I could ask but it is already too late. My body has resolved the dilemma for me. The voice from above says to introduce another plastic tube all the same. I have to stay very still while the medicine drips in that will scare away the phantoms. But they've already gone, departed, gone back there. I could follow their route along a dark spiral path. I could have taken another step in the dream – they wouldn't have been surprised. They'd wait for me tenderly, one of their own.

I wake up, purged of guilt.

It is morning, noon, daytime. I get bravely up out of bed. I go along the corridor 'weightless or as if weight no longer matters'. The neighbouring door is open wide. A young man is lying in the bed, propped up on pillows. He breathes raspingly, with difficulty. From the television screen a blonde is watching him, saying: 'Hawaii awaits you.' He smiles, as if this is perfectly obvious. In the corridor, the nurse brings the old Polish woman a tray with lunch. She slowly turns her head, listens to the footsteps, lowers the tray, raises the lid. The sound of the spoon dipping into the thick porridge. After the first bite she sighs with relief.

As the shower sprayed my face I took a deep breath, as if drinking moisture into my lungs, not just into my skin. I miss moisture in the air, in my eyelids flickering dry over the whites of my eyes, in the sheets, in the tips of my fingers. I stand still under the shower, hands by my sides. There is nothing to hold on to. Shoulders relaxed, my neck bends and I become soft and empty. From the outside: large drops of water bounce off the slippery wet body, fracture and pound rhythmically on the wall; steam; a crumpled towel on the floor; another over the edge of the bathtub; three spots where the enamel is rusty; transparent soap suds on the edge of the drain. From inside: the moisture penetrates and the skin spreads like an elastic membrane; the emptiness keeps expanding, an emptiness through which I can finally accept all this water, its flow; the water proceeds tentatively, as if it has a foggy memory of my resistance; that body is slowly changing, reviving. A memory of weight, a memory of lightness. And water – the sole firm, palpable thread that runs from inside out.

As I left the bathroom I felt festive. The fact that I had taken a shower filled me with courage in a special, inexplicable way.

I will re-establish my system. I will impose my own discipline on the hospital order. I will change from a nightgown into a sweat suit and exercise on the indoor bicycle until I tremble with exhaustion. I will take control of the medicine. They may not be careful enough, I shouldn't trust them completely, I must take control. I'll make a list and check my findings every morning. I'll catch the rhythm of sleep and only sleep at night.

I will reconstruct time. I'll fill the emptiness with fragments of conversation, newspapers, television images, news. News? What has happened? Olaf Palme has been killed. Unrest in the Philippines. This is not news. News is snowfall expected in the northeast this weekend. The dense sky is obvious on the satellite shot. A merry forecaster in a ski sweater points to a sketched cloud hovering over the names of cities. I still think it unbelievable that something like weather can be predicted, that it really will snow. From his cardboard cloud on the television screen big flakes are falling, larger than the round dots on the map marking the cities. It will melt on the glass and I will look at the snowy window. That is certain, it is almost certain, no more effort is required.

Paper flakes, like Hawaii.

I'll pick up a book and while I read the day will go by. Time will pass of itself. It will slide smoothly between the pages, I won't have to think about how it's passing. I'll fall asleep without impatience. It will be shut in the covers, it will wait for me to pick it up tomorrow, among the thin, yellow-edged pages that rustle as I turn them. Because I will no longer have to listen to the dry rustling as it echoes in space. I won't be aware of my fingers that turn the pages, my breath, the lamplight falling diagonally and stretching the shadows. The room's hot, slightly stagnant air. I won't have double vision, I won't really watch time flow, like milky fog in a dark inner space – horribly fast, whirling. Then dizziness would overcome me. I would have to put down the book, lie flat and breathe deeply. Or get up and spit out the bitter scum suddenly collecting in my mouth.

The book has a black cover embossed with silver letters: *Gorky Park*, Martin Cruz Smith. Inside three corpses lie frozen in the snow. Pages. Worn edges. The dull, worn outside. The letters uncoil across the icy skating rink, the park, young women, plaster models of heads, cigarettes smoked by investigator Arkady Ranko: a regular, monotonous sequence whose meaning I no longer understand, I simply watch it unravelling, faster and faster. Nonetheless I intend to read to the end without skipping a single line. How much time did it take to string these cyphers of flow? Eight years it says in the afterword. Looking back, the writer realised that eight years had passed. Before him lay a book. Paper, black print: time had truly passed. If it weren't there on the page, the writer thought, I wouldn't believe it. When I bend my head and raise it again, time no longer exists, except in the black letters, the thin, fragmented sequence. Suddenly weariness seizes me: time doesn't exist outside of me and I've given the time inside me to Arkady Ranko. On page 433 of the Ballantine paperback edition, Inspector Ranko leaves without knowing that behind him the last page is turning, that his life story has been written and that there is nothing to follow.

He couldn't turn around.

In the novel, thick snow was falling.

I will establish a balance between time outside and time inside. I will resolve the conflict encroaching forcefully on my consciousness, then immediately retreat. I will find a centre and from it construct the sequence on paper, the beginning and the end. It is wonderful that sentences have a beginning and an end, that their structure is unclouded. I will take down notes daily, a sequence of neatly ordered proofs of existence – disintegration, existence. I will draw a line, no matter what, fill the paper. Write. If words come out of me, if my handwriting becomes legible enough, will that help me? Will I then be more real?

Notes: start with the word I fear the most.

. . . death.

That five-letter convulsion. Carefully, fearfully, I write it at the top of each piece of paper, the upper left-hand corner of each new notebook, on the first line. Miniscule letters, hardly legible. The first letter lower case, although I hesitated for a moment thinking that it could be a capital. Surely it should be a capital letter. Not long ago I wouldn't have even stopped to think. But now the decision is no longer mine. It is in the hand that writes a lower case initial letter d, diminishing the word, diminishing the fear.

I will write out that word that I fear the most, name it and admit that it exists: it, me, my fear, its inevitability. And then I'll cross it out. With a childish gesture I'll make it an unrecognisable blob, pressed into the paper from the ferocity with which the hand pushed down on the pencil tip.

Nausea. I cannot write that word without nausea. The joints of my fingers are suddenly white, almost transparent.

I hesitate, as if I've never written it nonchalantly before. But now, writing about myself, the word is new for me. Like a man, I have never written about myself before. Why can I not avoid the word death? It has kept me company for such a long time that I am growing tired of it. But, as I write, past feelings, events unfurl before my eyes. Suddenly they pour onto the paper, they become the past. The feeling of exorcism: a nightmare emerges and becomes palpable, a thing, paper, letters, a spot.

Mastery over matter. Control.

What relief.

Everything is familiar now. The space, the mirror, water, the way that the cleaning woman empties the waste paper basket and folds down the edge on a new bag, the alarm bell, the menu, the television programmes, the weather forecast. 'Do you want to extend your television subscription a few more days?' a young man in a green military vest asks me. 'Seven days,' I say. 'I doubt they'll keep me here longer than that.' From the pocket on his vest he takes out a pad and writes out a receipt. He hands me the duplicate, a green piece of paper on which the copy of my name can hardly be seen. The gesture with which he writes out my name without a second thought, ripping off the slip of paper. A glance. How many seconds does the image last in the brain? The word 'receipt'. My name. Suddenly it seems so simple, like in a movie or a novel: the heroine makes a decision and obstacles become negligible before the force of her will. Her eyes take on a decisive shine, the self-assured hand fills an entire page with a single, repeated word. Then another. Then a third. For now this will be enough, the heroine thinks: dense pages of little black deaths, immediately crossed out. On some of the pages underneath marks remain – fainter and fainter. Then the heroine turns the dial on the phone a few times and each time says 'Hello!' in a pleasant voice. 'Yes, I'm fine. Excellent. No, in a few days. Yes. Yes. The incision is completely healed.' She discovers that it is very easy to telephone, to hear the voice of a friend who has vanished briefly from the horizon. To relieve them of their fears, freeing herself of their emotions which suffocate her because she is not in a state to return them. She'll see them soon, the forecast says that it will be soon.

Thinking 'soon' with a light, almost ordinary flick of the wrist she turns on the TV. The *Towering Inferno* was on and as Paul Newman makes his way down a burning stairwell to save two children, she suddenly drops off to sleep. At night she gets up and goes to the bathroom but her legs can't support her and she slips to the floor from the bed. As she lies there, captive, it seems like a bad sign, to fall down and lie in the dark, lost.

An unknown woman entered the room. Businesslike, re-sembling an insurance salesperson or a treasurer collecting late dues. Pale, pink skin, especially thin on the eyelids, almost as if her eyes see through them each time she blinks. Perhaps that's why she blinks so quickly. She wears no uni-form. A metal name plate is attached to the right-hand side of her grey pleated dress. She wears a small gold watch on her wrist and as soon as she enters she glances at its tiny hands – she is stopping only for a moment, no intention of staying long.

'I am a diabetes specialist.'

Does she expect me to say something?

'Your blood sugar level is high and it doesn't look' – her voice deepens, caution, restraint – 'it won't be going down easily, which means that the chances of you remaining a diabetic are fifty per cent. You will start with insulin injections immediately. You'll give them to yourself twice a day. Here, while I bring in the equipment, study this material' – she hands me two pamphlets and a piece of paper with the word 'Instructions' – 'and then we'll practise.'

To fall and lie down in the dark, lost.

One leaflet is called: *How to begin – administering your own insulin injections*. The first picture shows delicate women's hands with long fingers and orange-painted fingernails – the nails are not long, the overall impression is one of neatness, not elegance – over a washbasin and a stream of bluish water in the background. The hands hold a bar of Camay soap. The legend reads 'wash your hands thoroughly'. In the next picture the hands seem bony. They show you how you should rub the insulin bottle between your hands so that the liquid gets mixed up, but it must never – NEVER – be shaken. In picture number three I am certain that the hands are not the same woman. This fact disturbs me. Photographed in close up, the right hand holds the little bottle and the left one holds a piece of alcohol-soaked gauze. They look chapped and old. The skin between the right thumb and forefinger looks peculiar, strangely taut.

The camera moves back: she inserts the needle into the top of the bottle with her right hand. At the same time I see her bony knuckles, the thin blue veins on her wrist and the slightly messy cuffs on her sleeves. This is an older woman, a little careless in how she dresses. When she turns the little bottle over and extracts the insulin with the hypodermic – it says do it slowly, avoid air bubbles – the intricate veins on the inside of her wrist are very visible, so is the wrinkled, almost worn lifeline, the lines of the head and of the heart. Then there is a picture where it shows how you wipe the place on the thigh clean with alcohol and firmly squeeze a two-inch piece of the thigh between thumb and forefinger. Then another picture where the hand pokes the needle into the raised place. On the side is a sketch that explains that the shot is best administered at an angle of between forty-five and ninety degrees. The woman whose legs are showing is not wearing fingernail polish. Her thighs, half covered with a blue terrycloth bathrobe, are thin and young, like the thighs of a high-school girl. When she removed the needle and pressed down with the gauze on the surface of the skin, no dimple was left afterwards.

I worry that the dimple will stay on my leg.

The other pamphlet, *Selecting and Changing Places to Inject*, gives instructions on parts of the body where the injection can be easily delivered: the upper part of the buttocks; the outer thighs and lower arms; the stomach. You should change the place once a week. One shows that same high-school thigh and a piece of blue bathrobe, hopelessly lost in the surrounding diagrams. You can live a happy and fulfilling life with diabetes.

So it says at the end.

The nurse isn't patient. Her voice is gentle and quiet, but tense. Below the surface, under the dress buttoned up on her chest, under her skin, in the depths of her lungs, tension. I can see she is in a hurry, that she isn't giving me a chance to think. Ripping off a bit of adhesive tape, she sticks the page of instructions to the wall across from my bed. She writes my name at the top and the insulin dose alongside, then sits down beside me.

Very close.

She rubs the bottle between her palms, cleans the top, inserts the needle and extracts the insulin. I do the same. Entranced, I follow her rapid, precise movements. She straightens the pleat on her dress and firmly pinches the flesh underneath. I can't see her thigh, its form lost in the even folds of the cloth. Then the pink fingers with fingernails cut down to the quick take hold of my thigh.

'You try,' she said.

A drop, barely visible, quivering at the tip of a needle hardly thicker than a hair. I hold it up to the light. For the first time I see this thin needle with a droplet pulling away, slipping. My hands are completely calm. I am not afraid, no, but I can't do it, I can't.

I tell her that I can't.

'Try again.'

'Again.'

She gives me a crumpled towel so that I can practise pricking: the quick, short prick; pressure, done. She thinks I am afraid of the needle. 'Are you afraid of the needle?'

'No, really I'm not.'

The needle isn't the problem, my whole upper left arm is full of scars from needles the size of knitting needles or crochet hooks. 'I am in the dark,' I say, but she doesn't understand. The towel is already damp from the false stabs and her temples are perspiring. It is close in the room and it stinks of alcohol. My muscles are tense. Once more. Again.

Calm down, this is important.

When she says: 'Again!' for the seventh time her voice is just a touch too high, cracking.

I love her delicate eyelids, the way they flutter, the way they betray her. I don't want to insult her but I keep putting it off. I am putting off the feeling when the needle first pricks my skin, the thought that I'll have to get used to it, recall the instructions on how to hold the little bottle with my palms, how to insert the needle taking the best possible angle into consideration, that I'll have to look at the pictures on the leaflets twice a day. Close up, as if I'm a part of them.

Having all that to think about.

New. Unbearably new. I know I can't deal with all these new things, attacking me. I can't master them.

The nurse is talking about nutrition, about taking care of my legs, about sores between my fingers. It sounds ominous. Why is she talking about my legs?

I mustn't think of Marko.

His legs rotted for months, starting at the toes. They broke out in green and lavender patches. They were amputated. Later, he fell off the hospital bed one night. He was so convulsed with chest pain that he fell. He didn't know that he was on the floor. While still falling he saw terrifying white pain overtaking him, carrying him off. It was all over quickly. At least so it seemed to us.

We were grateful.

The day before, he had talked about going home.

Hawaii, going home, snow.

I have fallen and am lying in the dark, lost. I see the open door and light behind it and I shout. 'Shhhhh,' someone whispers, 'don't shout so loud.' Now my hands are trembling. The nurse leaves and turns off the light. Legs, weight in the legs, paralysis. There is no way out, not any more.

I am giving up, I'm tired and I don't care. Then at the same time, as if I'm split in two or crazy, as if this is some other woman that I only know a little and whose reactions I can't predict, I flip on the light, look for the little bottle, fill the hypodermic, wipe the skin clean on my left leg and give myself an injection. A tiny drop of blood appears where I pricked the skin.

An incision.

I add a tenth to my list of nine medicines: insulin, twice a day, eight units. Then I have some bitter tea with lemon, it is quite drinkable.

For the first time I am able to contemplate leaving the hospital.

There is no cause for alarm, merely caution.

The outcome must be positive.

It is not true that I can do nothing but sit on this bed and feel miserable.

It is true that I can do nothing.

That's impossible, totally impossible. Even if they were to tell me: 'You are out of danger, your health is perfect, you can go,' I wouldn't be able to. That is how devastated I am. This weariness. As if giving the injection, the strength to give it, was a last, exhausting gesture from which I'll take ages to recover. I don't ever remember feeling this tired. My occasional little victories crumble instantly and the triumph of will and discipline turns into an act deserving only contempt. Nothing has changed. Not the way I'd thought it would. A new life! To walk like a child, to overcome each millimetre of space a thousand times until you master it, until you feel that you've mastered it. So, I've made it to the end of the tunnel. I see the door and when the door opens I see that there is another tunnel and another door at its end. I already know that I'll open that one too and that there will be nothing but white light on the other side. Nothing, nothing more. I'll recognise the light.

How quickly the sweetness of victory has left me.

I'm worried by this fragility. The anxiety that surrounds it.

I used to feel nothing but disdain for the body, now I feel enmity. Disgusting helplessness. Immobility. Weight. I have no more patience for its tests. I hate it. Myself. The self-regarding icy consciousness that will not go away, will not leave me in peace. It supervises me day and night, watches over me as I wear out, guesses whether I'll submit, calculating. It measures the amplitude of my emotions. It tests the limit of my efforts. It won't allow me to look back. It erases memories too fast. It divides me from the past, my friends, husbands. It pushes them out of my field of vision. They are all burdens. Emotions are nothing but a burden. It treats me like a stranger: 'You can do better than that,' it says, driving me on and on. I pretend to be mad. I pretend that I can't see where I'm supposed to go. There ought to be some way of stopping that monster, tearing it out of me by the roots – only then could I . . .

Maybe it's still not too late.

128

I hate this hope that drives me to order a steak, two steaks, that makes me eat them methodically, slowly, seriously chewing. Good Lord, this is all so tasteless, so pointless. Yet I don't seem able to stop eating, like I don't seem able to stop breathing. And that hopeful state of mind – how deceiving! It can only observe, it doesn't supervise, it doesn't make decisions. No one supervises, because there is no centre. The self is made up of millions of invisible organisms, each with its own will, its own goal of survival, stronger than my own, stronger than my weariness and my longing to be still. They wear me out: maybe that is their strategy. Their desperate wish to survive makes my longing seem trifling, makes me trifling. Organisms with their own logic and rhythm; they cannot go any faster than I am going myself.

I will never 'recover'. Never.

The unbearable, slavish, self-devastating love for life.

An unquenchable thirst. A selfish passion that even hatred cannot mar.

The thought: that I would be able to accept the idea of never leaving here, of never seeing anyone. Only here am I safe, sheltered, almost held. Doctors and nurses enter, measure my blood pressure, temperature, take blood samples, carefully monitor my condition. It would be best to submit to them utterly, only then can I rest. I'll tell them that I have to stay. I'll explain that nothing else makes sense for me. No one ever really leaves here anyway – or any hospital, for that matter. I'll always be coming back. For them I'm just a feature of the closed system of disease.

In this limited world of the hospital I'll never be wrong

or responsible for anything. The limitation functions beyond our control, incontrovertible fate, it is pointless to struggle against it. The world becomes defined by a single, central point, providing a firm sense of identity, a sense of power within limits, depending on those limits. If I do get better I will no longer have an excuse. Unforeseen options will suddenly arise. I'll have to make decisions. I'll be threatened. Only then, because I'm healthy, will sickness really threaten: heart attacks, escherichia coli, viral meningitis, thrombosis, arterial sclerosis, necrosis of the bones, gangrene, cancer. Everything I was safe from while I was sick. Because I had that uniquely horrible disease, I felt I couldn't come down with anything else. It seemed statistically implausible, impossible; there was not enough room in my head for two such ailments.

But now, now there is plenty of room.

The disease has departed leaving emptiness in its place. The situation feels threatening. The threat will follow me everywhere – in the air, on the bus, in a stairwell bannister, in shops. It will lie in wait for me. It is merely a matter of time before something attacks.

Ana and I went to a supermarket this winter in the middle of the night, down near the end of Sixth Avenue. She stopped at the cheese counter. I waited for her by the stocking display, carefully studying the designs and colours as if having trouble chosing. Ana stood with her back turned, wrapped in a black wool scarf with roses that flamed purple in the glow of the refrigerator. It was warm and the voice of Frank Sinatra came faintly from the loud-speakers – was it 'Strangers in the Night'? I strained to hear but gave up and reached for a pair of stockings marked 'beige'. Just as I touched the cellophane, suddenly, out of nowhere, I felt a threat: if I move even the slightest bit, if I leave this store, if I buy these stockings, an accident will happen.

Through the shop window I could see the frozen sidewalk glowing dully. Beyond it the empty thoroughfare. I knew I couldn't possibly go out there, into nothingness. I froze, the threatening object with its mysterious, printed word 'beige' in my hand. Under the cellophane, neatly framed by black cardboard, the visible square of stocking was the same colour as my skin. Nauseous, I dropped the packet on the floor. Instant relief.

The danger had been sidestepped, for now.

Nothing happened. I wanted to look at some stockings but they fell out of my hand. I bent down and picked them up and then left. While we were waiting for the bus, Ana asked me if I was feeling tired. I shrugged. The sidewalk was frozen, but I no longer cared. We came home. Going home. Where to?

Wherever I go, I'll be equally lost.

I'll be standing in my kitchen when, out of the blue, without warning, I'll feel as if I don't belong, to what I see around me, what I stand on, what I live in. It is slipping away. I'll grab a leaf of swiss chard and clean it so vigorously that I'll tear it up. The long stalk will snap audibly. Then I'll take another dark green leaf from the bowl and slowly run my fingers along the long furrow on the stem, along the spine between the two halves, the thin tracery of white veins, the asymmetrical outline. Slowly, as if afraid that this piece of reality, the only one that reaches me, is about to vanish out of my hands while the memory of its separateness remains. Or I'll crush it with the weight of my newborn anxiety.

Nothing happened.

I used to be sick. Now I'm well.

At home everything will be ordinary, like before. Natasha will be at school. A cup of half-drunk coffee will be on the table. A vase of dried flowers on the top shelf will stand precisely as I left it when I went, as if no one dared to disturb the balance of the house and move it. On the floor, slanted, a long ray of sunlight will fall, rounded at the top by the window arch. The scene that I love: sunlight on the dark earthenware tiles. I'll stand there alone, feeling I'm sinking again, clamming up. The question stretches out before me like a desert: How long?

A question that I will not repeat out loud.

Fingers on swiss chard, unknown fingers on my neck.

'Don't move. Relax. I'm going to remove the intravenous feeding tube.'

Her touch is feathery, almost like a non-touch. The tip of the tube slides up and provokes a tiny, dull pain in the chest, or rather the unpleasantness of some pointy, foreign object travelling through the blood vessel. I feel her breath on my forehead, restrained, tense. In contradiction to the voice that whispers: 'Don't be afraid, it's nothing, everything will be just fine.' But her right hand is trembling and the trembling is communicated to me through the tube. Her breath withheld. Foreboding, a mistake might be made, blood could spurt out at any moment through the wide incision cut with a scalpel through the artery. The sticky, pale liquid that nothing will stop, not cotton, not gauze, not a towel, not the sheet. It will gush out unstoppable, as if it must, because the relevant decision was made long before – and this is no more than the realisation. What could I do? She thinks: Who could I call to stop it, to save this woman who is giving in, who is no longer putting up a fight?

Once more the fear.

No, the irrepressible horror.

We shiver with uncoordinated, opposing rhythms. Please, I say to myself, make that effort, just a moment more and it will be over, you'll forget it all: the effort and self-control, constantly forcing yourself. Think of something nice, I tell myself, unconvinced, ingratiating. But I can't think of anything nice. 'It's all over,' she says, grinning. She has slanted eyes. The rubber gloves' fingertips are speckled with tiny spots of blood.

If only someone could hug me. Reality has become too dense.

I dream that I've gone back to Yugoslavia and I have to look at some basement apartment that I've left in my mother's care while I was away. I want to sell it. As I approach the two-storey building I see from a distance its unrendered walls. Maybe it's not finished yet. The path is muddy, I remember being surprised by that. A blond man in a trenchcoat walks towards me, a friend, an architect, who warns me that the apartment will not be as easy to sell as I'd thought. She hasn't taken good care of it, she neglected it completely. Just then my mother comes up and unlocks the translucent glass door, like the kind I have on my Zagreb apartment. There is a stench of rot and damp. The walls are falling in, plaster is crumbling and we hop over bricks to stand on sand and beaten earth. There is no floor. I go into one room, a great white hall with a high bed in the middle. Father is lying on it. He watches me but says nothing, asks nothing. I am very small compared to the bed. I am not sure whether he realises that I've been operated on. I watch him and think, 'Has she told him yet?' I walk on by myself through the house, open doors. Everything is filthy beyond recognition. When I open the last door a vast square black hole gapes beyond it, bottomless. I imagine it might be an elevator shaft but I can't seem to remember whether this house ever had an elevator. I stand on the edge, with my left hand holding the door frame. For one long moment it seems as if the blackness is sucking me in. Then I wake up. I'm inside the blackness and plummeting dizzily, with all my weight, towards the bottom.

No, this is still a dream.

Then I really wake up.

'I've got to get out of here. Fast. Tomorrow.'

5

I've been at Jelena's now for two days. Everything happened
with dizzying speed. They took off my plastic bracelet with
the number. 'You are leaving this afternoon,' they said.
'Your tests are excellent. We have a new patient who needs
your room.' The doctors and I shared a bottle of Beaujolais
Nouveau and made a toast with our plastic cups. A little of
the wine spilt on the floor for good luck. Doctor Weiss told
me that I had woken up in the operation room. I opened
my eyes and asked in English am I alive. 'That's how afraid
you were,' he said. He had replied, 'Of course you are alive,
what did you think?' I smiled and drifted back to sleep. I
don't remember that at all. Then the cleaning woman came
into my room – I still couldn't believe I was going – and
started moving things around. I had to leave. I gave the
nurses the azalea and they put it on the computer in the
hallway. I waited for Jelena to come and pick me up holding
a sheet of paper in my hand with the list of medicines I
needed. I memorised their names and how often I was supposed to take them each day. Now I'd be doing it on my
own.

'Stick this up on the wall.'

'Yes, yes, of course, I'll put the sheet of paper up on the wall.'

I taped the sheet of paper to the frame of an exhibition advertisement, 'Cuban Poster Art 1961–1982'. The picture had a man whose head turns into a paintbrush stand. Next to the poster I put an empty sheet of paper on which I'll write down my weight and temperature each morning. I arranged my medicines on the bureau under the poster, it was almost too small to hold them all. To set up my own little hospital, a point towards which I'll orient myself in the room. This is now my room.

Jelena arrived to pick me up. I inhaled the sea air in front of the hospital. She said: 'We are going home.' Finally, somewhere I can breathe free and say: 'Home!' But the room has changed. The bed is too low. In order to get up off it I have to turn over onto my hip and push off with both hands. There is a draft from under the window. The rug gets in my way because my right leg trips on it. I still pull rather than lift that leg. The door doesn't quite close. The room smells of dust, and sets me coughing. Even when I open the window the dust smell is there.

That is the smell of this room, it can't be aired out.

I must get used to it.

While I climbed the darkened staircase, Jelena rushed on ahead with my bag. 'Go on up,' I said, 'I'll follow on my own. I have to start somewhere.' The wooden steps were paler towards the centre, with a little dip, worn from walking. A rotund little turned bannister is on each step, with a narrow handrail running along them. I clutch the bannister and don't dare let it go. Under my fingers I feel the wood, smooth from sliding hands, tiny holes from worms, layers of dust, glued with sweat in the hollows to the side, the patina along the top that shines like varnish.

All of a sudden I am five years old, in an old house on the island, playing on the stairs. I creep in and out and around the bannisters and slide down the handrail on my stomach. A smell of fresh fish wafts in from the kitchen.

Here it smells of fried fish and potatoes. A roast. Mushrooms. Bread. This staircase is crammed with years-old smells that have crept and soaked into the wood. They never fade completely. I could unlock the front door in the dark and recognise the house by its smell: apple pie, roast turkey, cranberry sauce, boiled corn. The smell of long-since fried chicken, cat droppings, varnish and a sweet, penetrating perfume that lingers here by the door, where a young woman with short hair just went in a moment ago. She had hardly gone in when the fragrance vanished to be replaced by the heavy smell of a dog that the man in the apartment across the hall had just taken out for a walk. He turned on the light in the stairwell and rushed out. A heavy pounding of shoes and scraping of paws were heard. A bare lightbulb on a long string lit up the stairwell in the middle: a hallway with two bicycles and baby carriages; high wooden panelling on the walls, dark and jagged towards the top. Outside the door the fragrance of perfume has left stand blue rubber boots. There are two cardboard boxes in front of the dog's door, and on the second floor is an umbrella without a handle and a heap of magazines.

In the kitchen, the table is covered by a dark blue tablecloth with tiny white lilies.

Dušan opens a bottle of Mateus and says we are having fish for dinner.

'Eat,' says Jelena. 'Eat, eat!'

Or 'Have you eaten?' or 'Would you like some more?' As if she doesn't know how to say anything else. She takes cottage cheese and apples from the refrigerator. 'This is good for you.' She doesn't talk about herself. She asks me to tell her about the operation and how I'm feeling now. I sit in the kitchen – this one, some other one – across from her, across from my mother, Hannah, Grace, unknown women, and feel as if I'll never be able to get out of here. Through the steamed-up windowpanes, the dishes piled in the sink, the oil sizzling in the frying pan, the chopped onion, the hum of the washing machine, the opening and closing of the refrigerator, the peeling of potatoes, water coming to the boil, the tail end of the news and classical music – we talk. We utter words that get lost along the way. We shout half-finished sentences, syllables, gestures, sudden screams, glances, silences, codes that designate concern, hurry, frailty, joy. With a secret language we express all the delicate nuances of loneliness and longing, as if it is all implied. We meet like conspirators and, over draining spaghetti, we talk about fear, about the meaning of it all. We don't say these words. They are suspended in the air above the table with the emptied coffee cups. One of us turns on the gas or jumps through a window. Leaving behind a tidy kitchen.

My mother's kitchen, so frighteningly clean.

Nina's kitchen: the dishes washed and draining, on a red

and white check dishcloth.

The narrow pine floorboards are worn away in front of the stove by Jelena's shoes. While she cooks, she makes so many pointless movements. She leans over, picks something up off the floor, shifts the chair, takes a lid down from the shelf, then leaves it all and walks quickly from the stove to the pantry. She studies the orderly glass jars with six types of pasta, beans, walnuts, dried green peas, plastic containers of various sizes, lids, yogurt and ice cream cups, laundry baskets full of waiting ironing. She's not sure. A moment ago she went to the pantry knowing exactly what she wanted, now she's not sure. It might be rice, or perhaps potatoes. The potatoes are on the balcony. She opens the door and goes out onto the balcony. Spinach is boiling on the stove. The telephone rings. She closes the door. She answers the phone. She jots down that she has to go to the dentist tomorrow and the dry cleaner. She clicks the little television on over the sink and starts sweeping up. The spinach is still cooking.

'When I cook,' she says, 'I think about all the things I still have to read this evening for tomorrow's lecture.

'I'm exhausted,' she says, and sits at the table. Exhausted by this doubleness.

She is never entirely here, in the kitchen. Her study is at the other end of the hallway overlooking the street. The desk is so neat, as if she were trying to wipe away every trace of breadcrumbs, greasy fingermarks and spilt drinks. Or as if she rarely sits there. Late at night she closes the door to her study, turns on the radio and then picks up the book *The Biology of Computer Life* and continues reading where she left off the previous evening. They had guests who stayed late last night and when she sat at her desk she only managed to read one page. She remembers that it was page 136, but that is all she remembers, the number. She fell asleep with her head on her book. She has to read page 136 again, but before that she also has to make a list of the food that she'll buy on her way home. The thought of food discourages her. She notices a cup of tea she made herself last night that she didn't have a chance to drink. Once more, like a few moments ago in the kitchen, she is overwhelmed by a wave of weariness.

From my room I hear Jelena turn the radio on low. She thinks I'm asleep. A hoarse woman's voice sings of love. The colour of her voice washes over me, the way it sings the word 'love', so desperate, as if she doesn't believe that anyone is listening to her. I fend off her sorrow and the way the lingering drawn-out sound of the saxophone makes me feel helpless.

Suddenly I feel that it is dangerous to be alone like this, without love.

Inner smoothness, through which everything glides, slides, drips, frictionless. There is nothing for love to hold onto. The slithering mass of shifting impressions penetrates all openings and flows through the centre of a hard, dark, petrified tube. Only music can fill it, corrode its walls, make them a porous, sieve-like fabric of longing.

Now I see that this room has been emptied, swept of all obstacles, like my guts, hollowed out.

All the useless odds and ends have been removed that just collect smells and dust, in which bacteria destructive to the flesh multiply with mad speed. There are no curtains at the window, no books on the desk. This is a sick person's room, slippery from being too clean. On the bare shelf, from where all scattered newspapers, papers, Dušan's blueprints, bills, porcelain figurines, candlesticks and flowers have been removed, completely outside the system is a cocoa tin, *Chocolat Damay Granulé, garanti pur cacao & sucre. Magasins de vente 31 à 35 Boulevard Sébastopol & 50 à 58 rue Saint-Denis.* The wreath of gold leaves along the edge has almost been rubbed off by the fingers that have opened the box, taken the grainy brown powder with a spoon, put the tin back on the shelf and then stirred the cocoa with milk in a porcelain bowl until it is fully melted.

Fingerprints would remain long after my sudden death. On greasy pots, shoe brushes, the breadknife, the sewing machine, the typewriter, the cupboards, the containers for flour, sugar and sweets: the fingerprints would be visible. It would be impossible just to wipe them away, as if they were grasping the objects, as if they had weight. My old clothes would remain. Old? Not really. Worn once, almost new. Whenever Natasha opened the cupboards the clothes would suddenly age before her eyes and she would see stockings where a tiny run unravels into threads in an instant; a sweater with several moth holes that I never got around to mending would fall apart at a touch; a coat, just dry-cleaned, on which stains would start to show; a white silken blouse would acquire a dirty yellow patina in daylight; a posh dress would start to crease and the smell of sweat and perfume would waft from the underarms. The buttons I planned to sew on, the warm underwear I thought I'd be wearing next winter.

Intentions.

The intentions would get to her, the unfinishedness, the death that always comes unexpected and leaves a momentary disorder in its wake.

It is impossible to round things off.

She wouldn't look at photographs at first, then, after a month, she'd pull herself together and open the drawer. She'd see that her mother doesn't resemble her in a single picture. For a moment she'd be tempted to grab the scissors and cut out all the faces and arrange them on a clean sheet of paper: there would be something elusive, unknown in each face. She would feel that what was missing on all of them was me. She'd think so for a while, until my gestures, the colour of my voice, the glances through which she used to discover the nuances of my moods and my anxious silence would vanish from her memory. Much later, that wrong face from the photograph would be the only remaining truth. By then the unopened letters (that would keep arriving for some time), the papers, manuscripts, my four talismans – all would be stuffed into boxes on the tops of the cupboards. Everything that I cared about, everything that was Me, would be stored in those boxes. Finally, all in one place, put away. The corners of Natasha's mouth would curve downwards just like mine did, but no one would know anymore that it is 'just like mine'.

Racked by coughing Jelena kneels and dips the rag into the water bucket once more. The water has cooled. She pushes back the chair and rubs energetically at the last stretch of dry floor. The rag is almost black. Then she looks around my room. 'What more could I do?' Put away the books, they are only in the way, they can't be wiped with a damp rag. She took up an empty box and laid the books inside. She shoved the books into a cupboard. It wore her out, I know. She didn't have to. Why did she do it, why did she care? I can't bear someone else's concern, I don't deserve it. Can't repay it. I'll never be able to repay her.

Pity, that's what she feels for you, you poor sick woman. She's sorry for you, nothing more.

It was easier for me to think that way or I'd leave, go anywhere, hide my frailty, my shame.

Now, I lie in my mother's home, hearing her wash the dishes. I get up, full of some undefined rage. I go to her. I say: 'I can wash the dishes, I want to help.' Finally I want to see her sitting and doing nothing, not knitting, not watching television. I tell her to stop working for me. She says: 'Oh, leave me alone, it isn't hard. You are sick.' She says it as if the disease is her fault, as if I'm sick because of her mistake or lack of caution. I see her gingerly moving her left arm, careful of the pain in her shoulder. But she washes. That is how she justifies herself, in her own eyes, in mine. I know the sound: she piles the dishes one on top of the other just a bit too loudly, so that I'll be sure to hear. The sound goes out the window into the shimmering summer air and reaches me, multiplied a thousand times. All I hear is the clatter, like a message: 'See, I am doing this for you, I am suffering for all of you, I am suffering for you, for you, for you . . .'

That sound won't be muffled. I hear it in the noise of

the rags wiping the floor. Following me.

But now they expect me to get better.

All at once, health has cropped up. First a word, then a landmark. I don't know when I first heard it used in connection with me. I think it was when they released me from hospital, but I didn't pay any attention. Then the word took root. Dušan and Jelena tell me: 'Now you are well.' Natasha asks: 'Are you well?' I begin to trip over health like a stone. This was supposed to be it, what I had been waiting for, hoping for. Hoping? That is not the right word. My hope was very concrete, a piece of someone else's tissue to replace my own. Further than that there was no hope, there was nothing. I was totally unprepared for health. How am I to know what health is? All I feel is a series of changes: my face, my stomach, my skin. I urinate, my wrists are puffy with blood, my thighs speckled with tiny traces of needle pricks. I can't put my shoes on because of the swelling. Every third day I go to the hospital. They take a blood sample and I sit in the waiting room for about an hour, leafing nervously through newspapers. The doctor says: 'Stop that, stop it! Think about how you don't have to go to dialysis anymore.' That is what others say, too. They telephone. They ask: 'How do you feel now that you don't have to go to dialysis anymore?' 'I still don't know,' I answer, and I feel they're startled, that I should have thought of it first.

Thinking of health in terms of a negation: I *don't* have to go there anymore.

I went there. My legs must have taken me there on their own. I opened the double door and went into the dialysis room. I cast a quick glance to check, as if hoping not to run into anyone, but the room was not empty. Nurses were already making up the beds, pulling the stiff sheets tight for the next round of patients whose names were written out on the grid on the blackboard. A blackboard, so practical. It is so easy to sponge clean the timetable grid and write in new names. The changes are frequent. I knew that at this time of day between the two shifts – I can still remember the schedule – there shouldn't have been any patients. I wasn't sure whether I could stand their glances, the diminished reflection of my figure standing in the doorway dressed in a grey running suit and coming in confused, somehow repentant. The figure wants to slip in, move by unnoticed, for it is now cut off from them by an invisible barrier. In the shining black of their eyes my tiny figure would be multiplied – and I would be lucky eight times over, sixteen times over.

In each pair of eyes. In each single eye.

They would look at me as if I was well. They would see the health I still can't comprehend. 'Come over here.' The nurse beckons to me. In a side room lies a man, here for the first time. They show me to him as if he were expecting me. His narrow, pale face is sideways on the pillow. He is wearing light blue terry-cloth pyjamas that leave his neck exposed. He seems vulnerable. He looks down at his stretched-out arm into which the blood is returning, mixed with water. The nurse's routine movements seem to insult him, the way that her left arm is resting on her hip while her right continues its work at the machine, without looking at the machine, without looking at him.

'Tell him that it's not all that bad,' said the nurse.

The man was about sixty years old, maybe. It is hard to guess, sickness uses you up. His skinny body lay under the sheet, abandoned, as if he had abandoned it, given up on himself. Only his eyes moved: from his arm to the nurse then to me. I don't know whether he expected something of me. It didn't look like it. I know that feeling of distance from oneself, how the needle occupies his vein and the thin, cold stream flows in. Blood suddenly pounds at his temples and his body is hit by a wave of warmth from the salt that comes into the bloodstream dissolved in the water. This will happen again and again. It is hot in that room, where I can no longer hear the sound of the machine. I can't tell him that it's not all that bad.

But I tell him: 'It's not so bad.'

As I'm saying it, I think the word 'bad' isn't a word that can encompass someone's life, anyway.

I would do better to tell him that there is hope, concrete hope, organic, within him, in the tissue itself, that he should submit to it, at the same time as smothering its existence.

I would do better to explain to him the metaphysics of the two realities, the vertical division, the way in which a glass column grows right down the middle of a person. Explain to him the system of turning off and turning on. He wouldn't believe me, I see that in his eyes. It is so hot in here, but I do not leave. I can't yet leave. It seems that I could come here every other day even now. Come back to convince myself that I no longer have to come back. I can oppose the two realities only by watching this first: how the needle slowly comes out of his arm and the nurse firmly presses that place at the elbow. Later, he will do it himself, without even noticing that this is the only way to survive. I don't want to forget this. I don't know why it is necessary that I remember it, but I must: the way the needle goes in, the way the needle comes out.

I'm already forgetting, it's happening. I can't recognise the dials on the machine. Only a month has passed since that early frozen morning in New York and already I can't tell what the dials that I stared at for six years are for. Arterial pressure? Veinal pressure? Pump speed? The temperature of the solution? I don't want to know, not any more.

Was I ever here?

Scars heal quickly, my skin forgets.

I see a thin inner veil cloaking those years, erasing my arrivals, the dials, the noises, my previous self who used to come here. I stand stripped of memory before my own eyes. I finally recognise the nature of my insecurity: such abrupt oblivion; images that fall into a void.

Keep them. Pull them out.

There is no air left in here. It must be like this in the belly of a submarine when it dives; heat from an invisible machine, air from an invisible machine, blood as well. Machines follow me. It is quiet in the submarine. All that can be heard is the muffled resistance of the sea as the floor gently rocks. The man's pale face on the pillow is clearly lit, but then the beam of light shudders, the floor rocks more wildly, it gets dark. I can bear the pain in my chest, but to see the fear that grips his pupils and colours his face white . . . He looks at me with eyes of fear and I can recognise it as my own. A grown man seeing it as if for the first time.

His eyelids are peeling off in dread, stinging unbearably. He can't stand to look at me. He watches me and I can see that it sickens him.

That bare neck, so exposed.

He is lying there feverishly thinking that he will never budge, never again. Much later he will discover that this is only the beginning and that the end also has its own course.

In his eyes, only in his eyes do I see what I am now free of. His terror sets me free.

In the morning, when I comb my hair, it falls out in clumps. My leg and arm muscles are all withered. They vanished along with the liquid.

I started losing four pounds a day. I think of it as simply draining out of me. The excess water first retreated from my joints where my bones finally showed, then from the other swollen places. All that was left were pouches of fat arranged stupidly on my cheeks, stomach and neck. I move around more easily. My legs still wobble and I have to hold or lean on something when I walk. After losing sixteen pounds I felt like I was melting away. When I lost thirty pounds, my voice became reedy. I knew that it was chemistry at work, reactions, medicines that got rid of unnecessary matter. Beyond my control. I couldn't entirely rely on myself, not yet.

The draining came to a stop after thirty-four pounds.

When I lift my arm to comb my hair, the skin on my upper arm sags, toneless, tired. I have grown weary of the sudden transitions, the lack of recognition. I am afraid for my heart. Will it be weakened by the weight loss? I call the doctor. 'Walk, move around, that is of utmost importance at the moment. I know patients who couldn't get up out of bed for a year after the operation.' 'But I don't know how, I'm all skin and bone.' 'Exercise. Go right ahead and exercise.' My clothes flutter around me, they slip down. I am so light that I am afraid of the wind.

I must go out, however.

Finally to take that step: 'out'.

I touched the doorknob. I feel like glass, like very finely polished crystal vibrating almost to the point where it shatters. As the door closes behind me I feel for my keys in my pocket. Although they were there, an unfounded suspicion arose that I might not be able to open the door when I got back.

The street has three churches and a funeral home with a black plastic portico from which letters are peeling owned by a B. Watson. If I set out along the left-hand side towards the square and the funeral home I have to pass an old people's home and a bar with SOUVLAKI written on it. There are two empty tables, a young girl stands by the Coca-Cola machine and, elbows planted on the bar, she stares, vacantly. Next door to the bar is a newspaper kiosk and an unpacked bundle of *Boston Globes* on the pavement. Then there is a long row of wooden, two-storey shingle houses painted grey or white with little front yards that end in a metal fence. I hold onto the fence. There is dog shit smeared on the red brick pavement and I have to be careful not to slip. Grey sand glitters in the cracks between the bricks.

If I go down the right-hand side I have to cross the street

and turn from the church with the protruding little tower on the corner opposite my doorway. I'd pass by the school playground where there are no children. Two blocks further there is a laundromat and next to it a low house which would resemble a barracks if it weren't for the words Computer Center along the entire white-painted glass wall. Through scratches in the paint I would see a dusty floor and footprints as if someone had meant to go in but before coming to the end of the room had changed his mind. It takes twenty minutes to get to the square, turn right, enter the Post Office, toss my letter in and come back the same way.

On my way back I feel less shaky.

The girl at the bar has moved. She has poured a drink in a paper cup for a tall guy wearing a cap with a visor. He downs it in a hurry then wipes his mouth on his arm. Caught by this gesture I look away, as if I've just seen him naked. Meantime, on the pavement undermined by weeds more sand has collected in a little crack, the same sand that I saw earlier. The walk has taken so long that a desert has accumulated on the pavement. I recognise the grains as if they were under my fingernails or my teeth, as if they were mine. Here, now, without hesitation, suddenly, the border between 'inside' and 'outside' is erased, the two realities are gone. With one foot in the crack and one hand on the crossbar of a fence eaten by rust, I breathe in the moist air, rain that is about to fall.

Here, now, completely present.

As if I've come home.

Cracks in the pavement. An upstand between the street

and the pavement where grass is growing. A crack on the façade under an open window. I hear a grandfather clock ticking. I know it is a grandfather clock because I have seen it, even though I'm not tall enough to see over the sill. How old am I? Three? Less? Tall weedy grass grows under the window, its leaves stick to the fingers. Bits of plaster crumble off and on the soles of my feet I bring sand into the yard of the house by the sea, paved with bricks like this, paved with bricks. In the middle of the yard is a water pump. I shiver at the touch of the iron handle. I stand there. The doorway is open, I can see the neatly laid bricks in the bright light. The cracks between them are filled with earth and sand. I try to hop on my toes from one to another without treading on a crack. If I do it will bring me bad luck. The hologram theory of memory.

At the door I take out my key. It is past noon and the street is empty. I push the key into the lock. The door won't open. The key is new, the brass still shiny.

I knew it. I can't coordinate movement and thought.

I begin to ask myself why, but give up immediately.

I observe myself too closely, as through a magnifying glass or a microscope. Then I zoom out, looking from a distance, as if from across the street. I seem to be constantly zooming in and out, in and out. But in fact I am doing nothing. A moment before there was a feeling of unity, but that was chance. Every day I must unlock the door, climb the stairs, do ordinary things in ways that don't wear me out, that don't bring me to the brink of misery. I can't bear this slow motion, the fractured feeling, the energy that I must invest in unlocking the door and the dread that it won't open. This constant fear that shifts from object to object.

I won't be able to get into the bath.

I won't be able to wash my own hair.

I won't be able to cross the street before the lights change.

I'll fall down stairs and lie at the bottom until someone finds me. It is so hard to enter the first reality, as it is hard to enter this house I know well, through the glazed front door. I even have a key, but something resists my entrance, my total transition. I am dragging some undefined burden after me, a blurred memory, things I'd rather not think about. If the burden were suddenly to fall away I'd embark on what is called my 'new life'.

If I could feel the tearing away, the snapping threads . . .

I hesitate between the desire for this freedom and the need to relive the indistinct memory and make the picture finally become clear. I think I can face it now.

A gust of wind rattling the windowpane wakes me up. It is still night. The heat is off. I snuggle deeper under the covers, right in the middle of the bed, darkness cooling around the edges. The middle of the bed sags as if someone had this same habit for years, lying on their right hip before waking, shoving their clasped hands between their knees and then laying there quietly, listening to the sound of sheet scraping shoulder.

I must have been sleeping in these sheets for over two weeks by now, more perhaps, but I need the dirt, the miniscule germs in the creases, the black crumbs from between my toes that stick to the fabric, the pillow greasy from my hair. As I lie there, bread crumbs rub my back. The edge of the sheet where I wiped my fingers last night smells of orange peel.

I nestle into dirt: I shape intimacy.

In the silence before dawn, I can distinctly hear the tiny flakes of dead skin falling off and filling up the empty spaces in the weave of the sheets, the holes between the tiny threads. A new layer is forming on the cloth, a light brown print in the shape of an egg, a body curled up on its side. When I lie down again I grow into my dirt so smoothly that even air can't come between us. This unquestionable presence in space is soothing.

Awakening comes from the street. I listen as it approaches: steps on the dry snow, a car motor in the yard, the squeaking of the front door across the street, a child's cry. The loud flushing of a toilet in the next apartment. And then a lull, before the house is flooded with footsteps, the patter of bare feet, morning news on the radio, voices that mix, the noise of gas on the stove. It is then, only then, that I try to remember. Touch, the safety of that touch. Reliance. The warmth of skin. I can bring it back: two arms encircle me and quickly pull me back from a brink. Distant, highly-attenuated images float towards me, emerge through silence in slow motion, and I see myself, very small, sitting in a boat, holding onto the edge with both hands. The boat rocks, I lean over to scoop up some water. My body is small and tan and my blonde hair sticky with salt and caught up in a clasp to the right. I can't see whether I'm in a swimming costume or not. The boat tips to one side and I see my face rippling on the surface, dispersing. The instant before I topple over I feel a touch. Maybe mother, maybe father, both are with me in the boat. Father wears a white bathing cap.

I don't remember this happening. All I can see is the event before me, far off, a faintly-lit fragment emerging from the darkness. The faces with their soft movements are barely recognisable. They come close, magnified and flat, then suddenly slip sideways as if they don't want to see me anymore.

As if they are ashamed.

I try to make contact, to calm down enough to get really close, but my movements, even the fluttering of my eyelids, everything frightens them. I replay the scene, stop it, reconstruct. It is painful. Lying in silence awaiting remote images. But they are too transient. I wake with a feeling that something is missing. Fortified under the covers I feel that I should be able to remember. It can't have been lost. It. Touch – once upon a time it did exist. I must start from that earliest recollection, from that face dispersed in the water. Touch. The intimacy of dirt, my childhood face, a memory that evades me, memory that binds me. I must remember everything, everything, everything.

I'll wait, curled up, as if cringing from a blow.

I'll wait.

Jelena brought in the letter with the newpapers, one of her bank statements and a Co-op flyer announcing bargains. The envelope was small, a little crushed and worn around the edges, the address handwritten. I recognised mother's hand. Not one of her life's shocks had changed its curves, the frivolous curlicues, the old-fashioned penmanship of carefully inscribed capitals. That was her – smooth, round, a curling form. I hesitated before opening it, dreading her words, how they will slip right past me while I, as always, search vainly for something more. The letter had been sent one month after the operation.

'Dear daughter . . .'

My name isn't there, no tender opening, just the strict statement of our kinship. She still holds to form. Any woman who read this might assume it was meant for her. The envelope is addressed care of Jelena. She might have opened it by mistake. Or it could have been delivered to another address. 'Dear daughter' – not me alone.

I *freeze* at the opening line, that cold greeting. At the same time, I know how it continues. I get such letters regularly, each almost identical, differing only in nuance. Their regularity is something to hold onto, at least. When I read her letters, I think about how she wants to say something entirely different but doesn't succeed. I know it all: that she is at the coast and that it is cold there ('but probably not as cold as where you are' – she admits that it is harder for me). Every day she thinks of me. She called Natasha but didn't talk much. She says she is waiting for me to come back.

My hands tremble.

She doesn't know what to write to me. She doesn't know what to say. She simply watches helplessly as if she has long since given up on helping me. Each time it strikes her that she ought to do something for me – write me a letter for example – she is overwhelmed by helplessness. Her letters travel, the papers arrive with strange, alienating sentences at their destination, and the reader is gripped by an inevitable sorrow. Departures, arrivals, celebrations, moves, misfortunes – they all evade her. She doesn't know what to write. She is grimly motionless, she waits.

Closing she sends me a kiss.

She signs off with no name, just as mine is missing from the greeting.

But no, I'm wrong, this isn't the end. On the other side there is a postscript: 'I am sending you a few violets. I found them on the path as I went down to the village. They are the first violets this spring, my favourite flower.' Underneath, attached with a bit of paper tape, the kind they used in dialysis, were five light-blue, pressed and dried violets. The image of mother climbing the path, noticing the violets, picking them and bringing them home. She takes the tape father brought from the hospital to bandage the needle pricks in the evening after dialysis. She sticks them carefully to the paper so that they won't break. Only then does she write the letter. She only writes it because she thinks that she can't send the violets alone. She considers doing just that but decides against it and dashes off a few words. She hesitated over the paper with just violets and judged it 'empty' so she filled it with words. In the movement with which these ordinary, dry words emerged from under her pen, I see my guilt. I didn't know that this woman, my mother, had a favourite flower. Why do I expect her to tell me? Why force her to say everything, to suffer? Am I punishing her? The fragility of the paper, the handwriting, powerless in its rigidity, the pale violets – they too are her.

Let go, I tell myself.

I hear Jelena in the other room, her voice on the phone. Outside a passer-by whistles, as if it is really already spring. I am sitting on the bedspread and on my knees another thin sheet of paper on which, in another handwriting – spindly, tall, self-assured letters – three more sentences were added. I don't recognise the hand. I look at the signature: 'Love from your old father.'

The whistling can no longer be heard, just the sound of the piece of paper slipping slowly to the floor.

After twenty years.

A piece of paper lying on the table in the living room, on the embroidered tablecloth, propped up on the ashtray so that I am sure to see it when I come in. A piece of paper torn from a pad, perhaps one of my brother's schoolpads, with thin grey lines and a single sentence written in the middle. Morning, there was no one home. When I reached for it I thought that it would collapse. On the paper in this same handwriting it said that I had to leave.

'Jelena!' I shouted. 'Jelena!'

She comes in.

'He hasn't written to me for twenty years,' I tell her.

I had to tell her. Then pain swamps me and awkwardly, because I don't want her to watch me, I lower myself onto the bed and turn my head towards the wall. Caught by the blow, unprepared.

A dark memory wrenches itself out.

Jelena stands and waits. She thinks she may be able to help me.

Father hated to be called an old man. In the photograph I like best he wears his naval uniform without his cap. He has a high brow and gleaming, brushed-back wavy hair. His eyes are large, luminous, but different: his right eyelid is lowered slightly so that the top of the iris is out of sight. His left eye smiles. He is young, with a beautiful wife, a son, a daughter – he has a family. He looks like Cary Grant. I leaf through the magazine *Filmski svijet* and tell him that he looks like a movie star. He chuckles, delighted.

The day before I found the piece of paper on the table all four of us were in the living room. The door to the balcony was ajar, the curtain billowed, a train could be heard. His voice was threateningly calm. During dinner a fight started, another one. I can't remember what it was that he wanted. He came towards me across the room. Mother, petrified, looked out the window at the tips of the poplar trees, into the yard and beyond. His eyes – the charming eyes from the picture – grew larger and larger. They spread before me as if they'd outgrow their sockets, as if their overcast blueness would eat me alive.

He struck me across the face. For a moment I couldn't figure out what had happened. My mouth was full of blood. He hit me again. I couldn't hear the train anymore, just his voice. Not calm. Unintelligible. Almost a howl. Mother closed the balcony door. I didn't defend myself. I stared at his vast eyes, so close. I noticed their pupils, rimmed with yellow, turning towards the door to the hall, and then . . .

Shrinking, suddenly growing darker, expiring.

At the door, my brother. In his hand a pistol. His small, determined face, crooked glasses, ears that stuck out. He was aiming the pistol at father.

'Let her go!'

His voice was high, a child's. I closed my eyes. I couldn't bear his solemnity, the weight of his decision. I heard the voice, there wasn't a trace of a sob in it. He held the pistol as if he knew what he was supposed to do with it. I had hardly even noticed him until then, my little brother. Suddenly there I was between him and father. At that moment he didn't know that it would stay that way forever. When I opened my eyes father's face was grey, scattered with ash.

'I can't remember it,' my brother told me later at his wedding. He wore a dark blue suit and without his glasses bore a striking resemblance to father in that photograph out of the movies. Father was already completely grey and bent by then, hardly reaching my brother's shoulder.

'No, I don't remember, really.' But he did remember.

'It was a little after my eleventh birthday. Sunday. I was scared by father's voice. He hit her, then again, and again. She was crying. I was afraid he would kill her. I couldn't take it anymore. I felt a weight in my stomach, I remember, like a stone. I found the Berretta in the cupboard, wrapped in a piece of white flannel. Father had shown me how to use it. I loaded the bullets. Through the glass door to the dining room I could see his shadow as he moved. When I opened the door I couldn't see anything for my tears, except that she was crouching on the floor by the door. I don't know where mother was. I don't know whether I wanted to kill him. I don't want to remember that part.

'Forget it,' my brother said to me. 'Why don't you forget it once and for all?'

The next day it was all over. I left and I couldn't come back ever again. Much later I used to go for brief, orderly visits. There was no mention of this, of anything. My brother grew up in shadow. My child was born. I got sick. Father got sick. But there remained a firm triangle that could not be penetrated.

Out it came, like the lingering howl of a dog.

Jelena is frightened. She puts her hand on my mouth. I clutch myself tighter, tighter so as not to fall apart, not again, no, no.

I whimpered almost silently, with a voice out of the past, from dreams, from the rocking boat.

Father thinks that twenty years constitutes sufficient expiation, that I have been punished enough for my disobedience. His hand descends and lightly touches my face: 'Love from your old father.' He never said that. It wasn't written on that piece of paper.

Now I am afraid. I keep feeling afraid and convulsively turn my face away. Turn it away from him. Again I wait for the blow to fall. I know nothing else. I see that he is not raising his hand to me. He is silent and his livid cheeks are in my eyes. There is no yellow rim to his pupils any more, his whole face is yellow, haggard, as if he may topple over at any moment. Here, before me, he is toppling.

He wants me to forgive him, I know. I am forgiving him. I see him again as he sits by my hospital room window in silence, as he raises his arm and passes through the wall. He is giving me a sign. Only now I realise that it was a sign. I shout after him: 'Don't leave!' I think that he hears me but maybe not after all. Will my distant, belated forgiveness be enough for him? Will his three sentences written in his same, self-assured hand be enough for me? Like a new message, a new piece of paper to find on the table: 'Come back.' But I have been hungry for so many years that nothing can satisfy me any more. Meanwhile men have passed through my life and I have gnawed them to the bone, seeking touch, safety.

Jelena is still standing there. She says: 'You chose your relationship with your father yourself, that is how you lived. What else could you expect?' What could I expect? I no longer know the answer to this question.

The face of a man as we ride the bus together towards Belgrade. I am sitting in the first row. All the seats are taken and he is standing behind me. In the mirror above the driver's head I see his eyes as they pass over me, as he equates me with all the other passengers. He merges me with the crowd. The night before we fell asleep holding hands. 'Like children,' he said. Now, in the bus, my emotions, my energy, my tension are proportional to the expressionlessness of his gaze. I'm suffocating. His gaze registers my suffocation, but it no longer has anything to do with him.

In a New York bar next to Lincoln Theater Josh leans across a round black table and takes my face in both hands. His eyelids are closing and it looks to me as if his head will drop at any moment. He comes closer. The bar is empty. Outside it is raining. Through the window with red velvet curtains I see how quickly the raindrops are slithering. Over his shoulder at the end of the bar I think I see another man who I happened to meet at this same place last year. We were drinking red wine then, too. He was squinting, a little tipsy. We talked about theatre rather than about politics. Both of them were entranced with the sound of their own voices. I only connect their voices through time.

When we left Josh shoved his hat down on his head and then we kissed, heedlessly.

Repetition, a type of relationship that replicates, multiplying according to an existing pattern. I know it now, sipping wine for the third time, a year later. I am sitting behind the same red curtains and wondering, like a complete idiot, whether my life would have been different if the pistol had gone off.

6

The longing becomes recognisable, palpable. It is surfacing. I know that it is here: when I drink I still fill the glass only halfway. I am cautious. I consider. I think about every sip. No, it is not thinking, but a trained sense of measure, without overdoing it. Though to overdo means nothing at all.

I ought to be drinking more – tea from a silver teapot, fruit juices from tall glasses rimmed with sugar, a slice of lemon, ice and bits of candied fruit – but it isn't easy. After the third sip the glass seems to put itself back on the table. Then I pour another glass full and drink again and count, glasses, cups, sips.

How much have I had to drink today? Is it enough?

Do I urinate enough? How much should a normal person drink and urinate?

I have lost my sense of measure, I have lost a true sense of proportion.

I feel every single sip of liquid gurgling in my stomach, lingering. The more I think about it, the less thirsty I am. I'm scared that the water will stay inside. In the evening it seems as if the bloatedness is growing, the pressure in my fingertips, the weight in my legs, like it was before a dialysis session when I could feel liquid collecting and accurately follow it spreading through my body. I go to the bathroom every few minutes, but only squeeze out two or three drops. I force myself to drink more and wait: it has to pass through me. It must come out now there's no room inside for more.

Practise drinking water, like everything else.

Why do I suddenly no longer remember? I ought to remember how I yearned for water as I swallowed saliva, tears, spit, while I moistened my dry mouth with a sip of lukewarm water and thought of the girl with the fountain on the rue des Ecoles. Now ever since I've not once felt real thirst.

Oh yes I have. That day when I went back to visit the dialysis room, then I got thirsty. At home I poured out a glass of water and drank it right down. All of it. It tasted of the plastic cup.

Water always tastes of plastic. That taste makes me cautious, as if the operation drowned my thirst, tamed it, satiated it once and for all and a new thirst has yet to appear.

Oh, lord, its the two halves again, one wet and the other dry. I can't establish a bridge between them in my head.

The system hasn't changed, it has merely been transformed: there is none of the anticipated, total solution. Very easily, with a single decision, I give up salt and sugar. Without regrets I get rid of everything obstructing my purposes, as if the taste of food – the pleasure – is entirely beside the point. That is a part of the system, ignoring the pleasure. I re-establish a hierarchy, having shifted the centre.

Salt. Pleasure.

In 1950 my Aunt Natalie spent Christmas on Capri. She sent her sister a large black and white photograph of the celebration. In it she is leaning against a wall in a formal gown, by a decorated Christmas tree. Her clinging silk dress glides smoothly over her curves. She wears black patent leather sandals, a gold bracelet on her right wrist and a gold watch on her left. The Christmas tree is decorated with shiny balls and glittering lights. Even in the black and white photograph you can see them glow: the decorations, the bracelet, the shiny patent leather sandals. I wondered what sort of tree it was and what that was glowing on it and why don't we have one, too?

In another picture taken in 1946, on some Italian beach, Aunt Natalie is sitting on the edge of a boat in a light-coloured, fish-pattern bathing suit. Her toenails and finger-nails are varnished. She is smiling. The war was only just over and she was already sunbathing on a beach. In Yugo-slavia in 1946 pleasure was still considered immoral. I wasn't yet born. Later, prohibition was still enforced, but by my father: high heels, lacy sleeves, lipstick. Now there is no prohibition but it is too late. Years of self-denial and re-pression have created a harsh mechanism that grinds up Christmas trees, nail varnish, jewellery, evenings on the town, salt, sugar, longing for love, longing for water, plea-sure. I give things up with frightening ease. I am never tempted to overstep the prohibitions. Perfect discipline. Perfect rigidity. Now and then I seem to hear the steel spring snapping. But no, my longing for life is endlessly flexible.

I am subjugated by longing, my ruling principle.

At the end of the street, there is a footbridge over the main road which leads to a park where students play baseball. Otherwise it is quiet. A dark and soundless river runs along it. I should go there every day. I should exercise my muscles, my lungs, my eyes, look at the tall buildings across the river and further. I should repeat movements, learn them by heart, so that I no longer have to think of them. I do it every day, it's my job. Nothing happens. Now it seems like nothing, but in fact my legs are firmer. I don't stumble. I think less and less about walking. I'm starting to run.

I run along the soggy ground. Black mud sticks to my sneakers. A flock of seagulls is on the path. They move over for me and I see how big they are, how curved and sharp their beaks are. As I watch one bird slowly rise and somehow awkwardly unwrap its wings, I have the distinct sensation that I am behind myself. My body is on its second lap and I am following it with my gaze, like the flight of the seagulls in the distance. In the gap between us I hear its puffing, the thumping of its heart, the wind blowing through its hair – and I feel the sweat on my back cooling off in an instant.

Not as it happens, but once it has already half happened.

Then I strain to reduce the gap. By the third lap I am sure that I'm inside, that I've got back into myself. I relax.

The gravel by the bench is clean. No longer listening to the footsteps, I just walk along and think: *How good it is that*

I'm getting so used to my body. The thought pains me, blinding, as if something is piercing my brain. Suddenly I notice black cracks between the grey pebbles. They weren't there before, they are spreading. The earth is drying, cracking. The abyss is growing.

I can no longer inflict evil on myself.

I can no longer think that way – the body that does this or that, the body that I am getting used to. The idea of separation is becoming unbearable. Like the idea that in some Asian countries, restaurant guests are served live monkey brain as a local speciality. The top of the monkey's skull is sawn off so it can be eaten with spoons. More than by the image of the open skull, the brain trembling beneath a transparent membrane threaded with slender veins, more than this I am sickened by the thought of the little spoon, the metal object, its slow intrusion.

Then the touch of warm brain on the lips.

The flavour of melting tissue.

Utterly limp. I don't want to be aware of my body, I want it all to stop. Now. I am worn out with changing perspective, the vividness with which I see myself, different every time. I am discouraged by fragmentation: eyes, hands, mouth, nose, ears, skin. Movements linked in slow motion, each clearly delineated in the mind, and only together do they comprise 'movement'. I no longer want to be my own audience, watching my life on screen as if it is someone else, pleased when some scene coincides with my own blurred recollections. I feel liquid, like plasma, never knowing which direction it will flow in, whether it will overflow, inundating its surroundings, unsure if it will find the

167

strength to creep back. Plasmic consciousness – this also is separation, a recurring hysterical awareness of the body.

When I sat on the stone wall by the square, across the street from the bookshop and the store selling sporting goods, I felt in sync with my surroundings for what seemed like the first time. The department store, the bank, the out-of-town newspaper stand, the subway entrance – I can take it all in. The passers-by are no longer a crowd, a kinesthe-tised, mobile mass that scares me. I can distinguish between them. I work at distinguishing between them, separating the face of a black man from that of his white wife, from their child in its pushchair, from students with backpacks, from an elderly gentleman who leans towards his wife and whispers something in her ear. A boy in a rumpled shirt is reading psalms out loud on a fence. A little further on, a one-legged black man is sitting and mutely rattling a beer can with a slit for coins. On the other side is a blind man and a woman playing with a Casio. They are sitting under a sunshade which gusts of wind keep flipping over. The woman gets up but, instead of closing it, stands it up once more.

In front of the subway entrance sits a woman in a wheel-chair. She has a blanket with black and green squares on it thrown over her knees. There is a sign in front of her in tiny, close letters. No one stops. The woman has a microphone in her hand and is singing. Her voice echoes through the square, bounces off the bank and disappears down the subway entrance. Then it returns to her like a jumbled, drawn-out moan. She shivers. Watching a young girl with long, flowing hair run down the steps, the woman thinks: 'That is real life.'

'Real life,' a man says in a subway car as the train pulls out of the station. His grey coat is unbuttoned. He says it to a long-haired woman in a ski jacket who vaguely nods her head. I am standing next to him and can clearly hear his tone: it sounds like an insult.

If he says that once more I'll rip out his Adam's apple. I'll bite right through his exposed neck and feel his cartilage between my teeth. I'll yank on the Adam's apple until I can hear it tearing away from his lungs, until the gurgling stops.

If he speaks, I'll kill him. I hope that he won't resist. I'll shove a finger in his eye. I'll cut off his tongue or, quite simply, I'll slit the artery in his neck and let the blood ooze out and coagulate on the subway carriage floor. I'll wait and then get out when it's not slippery anymore.

Hit. Hit blindly. Hit with pleasure.

I have never hated anyone with the intensity that I hated the man on the subway who left without a word when my staring at his Adam's apple became too heavy.

'Mister,' I wanted to say, 'there is no such thing as real life.'

'Real' and 'unreal' don't work as categories here. If there had been emptiness there instead of a station, if he had stepped through the open car doors and strode into nothing – and if someone had pulled him back in just as another train arrived from the opposite direction – he would never again have mustered the strength to say the words 'real life'.

It is sickening how sensitive I have become to words. They make me feel responsible, as if aimed at me alone.

While they are still in the air I judge their weight and watch with horror as they fade and grow transparent. I dissolve them with a glance, as with acid. Images arise behind them, three-dimensional, moving scenes. When I hear myself say 'acid', I see the word falling through paper, eating at it, and a hole is left in its place.

I open the paper at the page where there is a story about a taxi driver who ran over a man in an accident. Hesitating, I quickly scan the lines then put it down. It says the man cracked his head on the sidewalk leaving a bloody smudge on the kerb. Bloody smudge. I see an oldish man rushing over the crossing, thinking he's made it, running. A yellow taxi approaches. The driver sees the old man and doesn't slow down because he expects him to make it across. A passenger in the taxi leans towards the driver and opens his mouth, thinking that he'll say something, warn him, but just as the voice is climbing towards the throat, the taxi sinks without resistance into something soft. The sound of the skull cracking on the kerbstone – 'bloody smudge' – can be heard as can a voice – the taxi driver thinks it is the passenger's voice – a short, surprised 'Oh,' maybe just the 'h'. The sound with which one dies.

I listen to a radio interview with a painter who has gone blind. Two young men broke into his apartment and tossed paint thinner in his eyes.

'I don't want to adapt,' he says. 'I don't want to use special stairs or vehicles or buildings for the blind.'

'Do you still have some hope?' asks the reporter's voice.

'For what, that I'll be able to see someday? . . . Ah, you thought I could adapt?'

170

'Yes.'

'No,' says the painter. 'I won't.

Then he talks, about how in his life – his life before – he had hardly met a single blind person. 'Where are the blind people?' he asks. 'There are so many. Where are they?' And he keeps talking, about how his worst fear is of the dark. He lives in the dark. He lives in fear.

I will never completely free myself of the nearness, the intimacy, the recognition of death. Even the word, the ability to visualise it: how the old man's head cracks flat against the kerbstone, seeing it come closer, at the same time hearing the sound of the crack and the hissing of air in the lungs that suddenly erupt with blood from the mouth.

They toss the paint thinner into the painter's eyes. He turns. His eyes are wide open. He sees the man's face, almost a boy, the hand holding the paint thinner. The hand swings, he tries to duck but the yellow liquid is already on him. Pain. His eyes are still open, but only enough so that he can see the room gradually fading. In the hospital he keeps seeing a bright white light, then the dark that drives him mad. He thinks he sees light. He is utterly alone in it.

Suddenly *all* words are threatening.

I suppose I should finish with them, not utter them, not name them, especially the key words: disease, body, system, fear, death. It becomes impossible to use them. They appear out of nowhere, multiply, then descend upon me and swallow me up, leaving weariness and devastation in their wake. I must end all this, not speak, not read, not think in sentences. List only blurred, undefined impressions, without trying to observe them eluding me. Arrested, labelled, they'd vanish into thin air anyway.

Instead of keeping silent I talk. I know that I shouldn't. I can't stop. We sit in a restaurant. Through the large windows overlooking the yard I notice a slender tree that is in bud. The day is so clear that you can distinguish the tiny wrinkles around the eyes of those who walk by. We are drinking bitter espresso, Hannah staring beside me. Her gaze covers part of my right shoulder, half my face and the window. I am saying what I don't think – worse, what I don't even want. Things come bubbling up to my mouth, who knows where from. I tell her about dreams, urgently, as if something essential depends on it. Or as if, if I stop talking, all those images, all the nausea, will stay inside me.

I tell her that I can't sleep without pills.

I lie there and listen to the house go to sleep. The silence grows. I'd like to fall asleep, but if I don't watch out I'll be back in the cold operating theatre again. They have given me the injection and I am just about to drift off. I'm completely limp from the struggle. My muscles rest quietly, not trembling. They have already surrendered. I feel rubber strips and buttons on my limbs that have attached my arms and legs firmly to the table. I hear my breathing – it suddenly becomes very noisy and far away – and the thin tinkle of metal clinking against metal. The dizziness grows like a light, gentle spiral. My eyes are already closed. I clutch the nurse's hand and a moment before the last vestige of consciousness vanishes I know that I will lose something important. I give up with a feeling of peaceful sorrow.

I tell Hannah that I'd cry out otherwise, I'd start to sob if I didn't lose consciousness instead. I tell her that when it happens again I have to take a pill. The dizziness is sometimes so powerful that I have to get up in the middle of the night and throw up. Leaning over the toilet bowl I talk to myself like a little child: 'It's over now. You've woken up. You aren't there any more, it won't happen again.' But the void remains. At the moment of submersion I lose track of time which, until then, has been flowing unchecked. I'm losing the sense of unchecked flow.

When I woke up it wasn't a sequel. Time wasn't passing. It wasn't standing still either. It was even. I woke at the centre of a flat surface on which everything exists in the same way. Including me.

Close and far are all that exist on that surface.

'Can you imagine that?'

She says that it's frightening.

No, but the dreams are completely different from before – so vivid, dangerous. Before it was me dreaming. Now I am also inside and it might happen that I don't know how to shift from one level to another. When I enter, I am constantly fighting. It isn't pleasant. I have no time to feel pleasant. I strain to complete my task. I telephone. I have a message to deliver but the number is busy. I call again. It is busy again. I stand in a telephone booth. What I have to say is important but I can't get through. Something is stopping me in everything I want to do. I'm supposed to organise the liberation of a large ship. I am in a group of several people. We are armed and the ship is sure to set sail if we don't organise our attack. But everyone abandons me, scatters. I lie on the deck, maybe I'm wounded. I don't feel pain. I throw away my pistol and shout: 'I don't need you!'

'Dreams like that are called nightmares.'

Hannah says it slowly, so I can understand completely. And she keeps staring over my shoulder.

'It does no good for you to tell me that. These dreams aren't called anything at all, not even simply "dreams",' I reply. And even more earnestly, even faster, I tell her about the tunnel. I dream that I'm underground. I have to dig a hole to the surface because I'll soon run out of air. It is so dark all around me that I can't even see the walls of the tunnel. I grope along the sticky earth, stones, roots. Suddenly I remember that I have a miner's lamp attached to my head. I turn it on. The lamp casts a narrow beam of yellow light on my feet. Only when I stand up straight does the beam light up something resembling a short, dispersed bit of path which trembles like a live thing from the pounding of the blood in my temples. There is very little air, only enough for a few more sighs.

'Only a few more sighs.' I say it with a clear voice as if I am awake.

Then I wake up out of breath and sweaty. Several times during the day I remember that no one came to help me.

I tell her that I'd like to think of my dreams as 'mine' and that they are symbolic, but I can't. They exist, I enter, then I dig, or suffocate. I really suffocate. I sob, the pillow is wet in the morning. It is hard to analyse something so real, a state which I enter and to which I equally belong. I could stay there. Perhaps that is what will happen – I'll simply stay on there.

174

The branches of the tree in the yard are perfectly still. The day is crystal clear.

I am not sure whether I want to go home to Zagreb.

'I know that feeling,' she says, 'but you do have to go back. There is nothing to tie you here. Natasha is there.'

With an uncalled-for ferocity I reply that Natasha is already almost grown up.

That is not what I meant to say. I meant to say that when a person exists on a level – on levels that are lined up one next to another without any order – here and there are only issues of perspective. She is close. She is here.

I also tell her that I'm well – I'm well for the first time. I say the words as if they hold my only plausible justification. It took a long time for me to be able to sit like this and rest my head on a cold window. A year, six years. I don't dare lose this safety. I'll lose it if I leave. It is dangerous to leave.

'It is dangerous to stay,' says Hannah, as if this is obvious and unrelenting and there is no point in speaking of it any further.

But I hadn't told her everything.

I couldn't tell Hannah the dream about Natasha or even utter her name. Hannah was the one to say her name: 'Natasha.' That way it was bearable. If I had said it, I would have felt guilt, so vast that it is best left alone, untouched, so that it won't suffocate me.

Natasha appears in dreams. I have come back. I look for her. She is not at home. I call her friends but she's not there either. The fear that I won't find her grows. I walk along the street, trees along each side. I stop by a group of boys and ask: 'Have you seen Natasha?'

One of them points to a long grey limousine with darkened windows gliding along the kerb. It stops, the driver leans over and opens the door. I recognise him but can't remember his name. The limousine has only two front seats. There are five or six young people lying in the back. They seem dazed. They are strangely neatly dressed: black trousers, black leather jackets, belts with silver ornaments, gloves. I am startled by their neatness. In the back of the car Natasha lies next to a girl who looks a great deal like her. Both are dressed in ceremonial black. I crawl over to her on my elbows, creeping among the reclining bodies. Natasha's face, framed by dark hair, is incredibly pale. When she sees me she whispers: 'Mama, we all decided to fly.'

At that moment, in the dream, I start to scream.

I wake up sobbing, my cheeks wet.

I couldn't tell her everything – how I notice a sudden flurry of movements. My departure is already in train. I thought a decision would be necessary, but no: signs of acceleration crop up of their own accord, concealed signs of intent. I collect my things around the house. Shoes, scarf, underwear drying on the terrace. Jelena does not stop me. My gaze out the window is the gaze of someone already a little in Zagreb, someone who looks out the window of her room on the ground floor to watch people walk by, darkening the scene. A shadow falls on the book she is holding and that soothes her. The things in this house, the house itself, become transparent, just as words do. Looking through them I can now make out another street, an avenue of chestnut trees.

While I sit at Jelena's kitchen table holding a translucent

porcelain cup with a delicate handle with a little leaf on top
and a flower on the side the same cobalt blue as the saucer,
I see a row of majolica cups hanging over the sink in my
own kitchen in Zagreb.

Jelena's house is collapsing. Or rather dispersing, as if
these aren't walls around me, but curtains. They pull back
without a touch, noiselessly, painlessly. They carry me into
a room where a little dog drowses on the rug, curled up
into a circle, breathing steadily. I walk through the
neglected garden, open the door, and before I close it I
register that I should trim the grape vine.

There was no way to tell her, no way of telling her about
the hospital where I sat opposite a man and a woman while
I was waiting for Doctor Weiss to examine me. The man
might have been about my age, his face treacherously grey.
They talked about an operation. I didn't want to listen but I
heard.

The woman said: 'It seems an awful risk to me.'

The man didn't say anything. He stared at the floor in
front of him. There was something stiff in his movements. I
clenched my teeth: she shouldn't have said that, I thought,
but it was too late. His fear surfaced suddenly, spread
through the waiting room. He couldn't hide it. He lifted his
head and, by his expression, he seemed ready to give up, as
if he could only be sure while he stared down at the floor,
as if all his decisiveness lay there, in front of him, at the
point where he fixed his gaze. Droplets of perspiration
appeared on his upper lip. He took a handkerchief from his
pocket and wiped his mouth and forehead. Then he took
off his jacket and slowly went over to the coat rack on the

other side of the room. The fear kept spreading behind him. When he sat down again, he described signs on the floor with his foot, indecisively, until he found that point again.

I knew that he'd lie in that same room with the yellow tiles, that he'd perspire more and more and all the while the word 'risk' would ring in his head like a judgment. He'll fall apart in there, in that room, long before the knife touches him. Fear will flay him long before that.

I can't watch it any more.

In advance, I recognise his – their – suffering, each shiver that runs down his spine, each twinge. Between them and me there are no barriers. We are all so dreadfully naked from the disease. It has destroyed every distinction. Our bodies and feelings have begun to merge, because we are no longer human beings.

I can't bear it any more.

I don't have to bear it any more, I am different now. Different.

'I am different,' I say.

He doesn't even raise his head.

I'm so tired that I have to lie down on the bench and close my eyes. Quickly, like something I have memorised, feelings emerge, concentrated feelings: such extreme excitement, such awful solitude that no one will be able to penetrate it again.

I am defeated by the fact that I still have no way of defending myself.

Doctor Weiss pats me on the shoulder, satisfied.

'You can go home now.'

That 'home' sounded ordinary, untouchably ordinary.

Natasha met me dressed in black.

I see her pale, tense face beyond the glass of the airport waiting room. She stands there calmly, the waiting room almost empty in the early morning. A man walks by and turns. 'How beautiful she is,' he thinks. Such a strong, alarming beauty, already determining her fate.

'How beautiful she is,' I think, as if seeing her as he did, in passing.

She approaches the glass.

I stand in line for customs. In between us perhaps ten metres of empty space, a blue painted floor and the glass. Her eyes under darkly shadowed eyelids search the queue unhurriedly, as if she wants to be perfectly sure. She still hasn't noticed me. Now she'll see me, now. The gleam of recognition. Contact. A lopsided sense of heat flooding my right side. The part of me facing her glowing, pulling warmth away from the out of sight half, until I tremble. I watch her green gaze move, come closer, see it slide across the face of the man in front of me, then over me, hesitantly touching my skin.

It lasts less than a second, a blink of the eye.

Her gaze passes on, doubtful. I feel as if I don't exist.

Or as if I was out of sync with my existence. A momentary disappearance: I plunge into the void.

She smiles, confused, and waves to me.

She shouldn't have been waiting here. Every possibility for confusion should have been eliminated. I could have come into the house, opened the door of her room and woken her up. To see her sunken into the pillow, with no make-up, like a child. If I'd come upon her sleeping it would have been as if I'd never left at all. For her it might have seemed that way. Not for me. We'd pretend that it had been that way: a door closes – a door opens. Departure. Arrival. I'd simply say: 'Sleep, stay in bed, nothing has happened.' I'd say it again, in a mindless desire to protect her. Meeting this way I won't be able to conceal the truth. We are both equally exposed to it, now, like radiation or white neon light. As she takes the heavy suitcase from my hand, it seems as if I'm stumbling, that I'll fall. The removal of that burden makes me utterly helpless.

Natasha catches me by the arm and hugs me firmly. She is so much taller than me that she could lift my feet off the floor and whirl me around in a circle.

'Mama, Mama,' she said, as if surprised, 'you've come.'

In her voice I recognise her own fear, the tiny, nasty, curled-up animal sharpening its claws on her throat. It is coming out now, that little beast, through the too-high, cracked tones that seem like quiet sobbing. The carefully drawn black line under her eye melts. With decision she picks up the suitcase and carries it towards the bus. On the bus she leans into my face: 'You are so strange!' But it is no longer important. In her eyes I am as weightless and luminous as a cloud. On the way home the bus drives by heaps of ice on the sidewalk. The muddy patches melt slowly and little streams spread along the asphalt. 'Spring,' I say, and it feels as if I've arrived somewhere.

*

The house smelt of age.

The changes were miniscule, scarcely noticeable. A wave of the hand stopped the camera. Then when I stepped into the frame again it was over, something had passed. Touching the table I felt a layer of the finest dust under my fingers. It had collected on the upper edges of paintings, too, on the lamp, under the stairs.

A few repairs were necessary: replace the shower head in the bathroom; buy some new glasses; one of the potted plants – a climbing vine in a glass pot – had dried up; the damp stain on the bathroom mirror had spread. I went from room to room and corrected the objects: the order of the tea cups, with their handles that should be turned to the right; the towels – first the large one for the bath, then the smaller, and the smallest on top; I scraped out the burnt saucepans; I straightened out the carelessly laid rug whose edge was not parallel to the floor tiles.

I did this for days.

Then I changed everything around.

At last. This is the first reality, the one I was longing for: round, simple, like buying things in a shop, like the way home, music, the newspaper. But the other reality intrudes and finds its way inside and there is no whole. In conversation with an acquaintance I don't listen to what he says, I just watch. When I think that I'll have to retell the conversation to someone else, I suddenly can't remember anything. I had only his face before my eyes, trying to conceal its excitement; wrinkles around the corners of his mouth; he glanced sideways at the table and grew pale.

Fragmentation again.

I feel like a person whose life has been chopped into little pieces. A dog's pink underbelly covered with sparse hairs. A head of cabbage lying heavy in the hand. A friend opens his mouth, hesitates, speaks. I can't understand.

I laugh and while I'm laughing I think that I shouldn't but carry on all the same.

I start dreaming again. There is a war. Soldiers attack with arrows. I stand on a balcony. They don't hit me. Suddenly my chest is wet. My throat has been slit, cold air enters the cut. Beneath the balcony flows a river. I jump in and swim with quick strokes to avoid the arrows, although I'm aware that my throat is slit. War again. Tanks pass through the city. A girl in a white summer dress runs down the street with arms spread wide. A tank runs her over. On the pavement all that is left is a pale print, the dress, hands, without blood, as if she's been ironed.

I awake lying on my back with my mouth open. In the evening I walk around the house putting all the knives away, even if they're dirty. I can't bear to see knives. Or shards, or razors, or the edge of a delicate empty glass. I see clearly that, instead of by disease, I am inhabited by a fear that I can no longer resist. This is my fear. I recognise it now, as if I have suddenly come close, while swinging on a swing, to the face of death. And then just as suddenly swung away. I remember that blinding whiteness, the dizzy mixture of submission and resistance and the brief moment of balance between the two.

I go up to the cosmetics counter at the chemist. I thought I needed something. Powder? Lipstick? No, I don't need anything. I force myself to buy some lipstick, but don't even open it to see the colour. Just then it occurs to me that I ought to lose some weight. The thought is retracted instantly, buried, like a *sin*. I unscrew the lipstick and, seeing its delicate, pink colour, despair overwhelms me. My hands are limp and I have to put my bag on the floor.

What more do I want?

What more do I want? I ask myself, as if longing had limits. I close the shiny black box and put it back on the shelf, putting away my own weakness.

At the supermarket checkout I glance nervously at my watch. It is three o'clock already! The woman in front of me takes the things out of her wire basket with slow, rhythmic movements: Solea soap, a bottle of mineral water, a round loaf of bread. I am captive in expectation.

Time, like a shiver of nervousness, traverses my muscles. A rush. A wave. Why am I hurrying? What am I supposed to be doing today at three, at four? But I am supposed to do something. Grasp it firmly, everyday life. I'll find something that I should be doing and hold onto it tight.

Now the woman is arranging the things in a brown, imitation leather bag. The plastic has worn away from the handles and the naked fabric shows. I shiver at it, as if someone was rubbing sandpaper across my skin.

I am alone. Skinned like that.

How much time has passed?

One day in the street in front of my house a neighbour stops me. She is old. The fingers of the hand that taps me on the shoulder can no longer straighten. She says she always knew I would win, because I am brave. Her touch summons the now distant memory of the hospital bathroom, the moment when the water began to flow out of me unchecked.

So distant now.

Returning to my room afterwards I stepped into another time. I clearly recognised the moment of transition and the cusp between them. I found myself 'here' the way you find yourself in some fantastic but well-known domain. Suddenly everything leading up to that moment of transition becomes unreal, unimportant. One feels only this, oneself, here, finite. You think that this is the haven you have been longing for. The 'there' gets lost, destroyed. 'There' is on the distant edge of a plain obscured by milky fog.

Finally it is no longer necessary to wait.

There is nothing further. Nothing more can happen, I thought, light, almost joyous, as if the future was a burden I had just shrugged off.

Suddenly the word 'courage' seems like a set of heavy, wet clothes that I should take off, that no longer belong to me.